PRAISE FO[R]

'These stories of reflection and resolve are all you'd ever want in a collection. Its crises are acute, and the thoughts and actions of its characters will cut to the heart.' Gavin Corbett, author of *Green Glowing Skull*

'Lucy Sweeney Byrne's stories are like songs that make you sit up and listen till the last note. An album full of hits, *Let's Dance* is sweet and catchy, tender and acid, salty and wicked – and always wonderfully readable.' Rob Doyle, author of *Threshold*

'Essay, autobiography, historical document, screenplay, historical novel, absurdist theatre – all have been worked into the short story, refreshing the form, keeping it unruly but not uncontrolled, allowing us to demand more from what we read. I don't know how she does what she does.' Tim MacGabhann, author of *How to Be Nowhere*

'In her gripping formal efforts to dilate "a passing something before the nothing's void," in fierce commitment to her subjects of time and the body, abjection and freedom, Lucy Sweeney Byrne is our Irish Duras while also wholly, electrifyingly, her own artist in every step of *Let's Dance*.' Mary O'Donoghue, author of *The Hour After Happy Hour*

'*Let's Dance* is a soul-stirring collection, as Lucy Sweeney Byrne carves women's simmering rage on the page with tender, hypnotic prose. *Let's Dance* is a modern masterpiece of the short story form. This collection is a triumph that cements Sweeney Byrne as among the best in contemporary Irish literature.' Aimée Walsh, author of *Exile*

Lucy Sweeney Byrne is the author of *Paris Syndrome* (2019) a short story collection, published by Banshee Press, met with critical acclaim and shortlisted for numerous awards, including the Edge Hill Prize, the Kate O'Brien Award, the Butler Literary Award, and the John McGahern Prize. Lucy's short fiction, essays and poetry have appeared in *The Dublin Review, The Stinging Fly, Banshee, Southword, AGNI, Litro, Grist, 3:AM* magazine, and other literary outlets. She also writes book reviews for *The Irish Times*.

Let's Dance

Let's Dance

Lucy Sweeney Byrne

First published 2024 by Banshee Press
www.bansheepress.org

First edition

A CIP record for this title is available from the British Library.

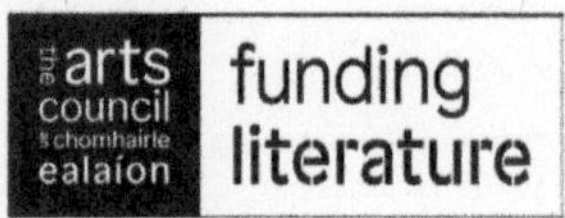

Banshee Press gratefully acknowledges the financial assistance of the Arts Council.

ISBN 978-1-7393979-7-5

Versions of these stories previously appeared in the following: 'Night Classes' in *Brick Lane Bookshop Short Story Prize: Longlist 2020*; 'Let's Dance' in *Banshee*; 'Gymnastics' in *Grist*; 'The Debutante' in *The Dublin Review*; 'To Cure a Body' in *The Stinging Fly*; 'Land of Honey' in *AGNI*

Set in Palatino by Eimear Ryan
Cover design by Anna Morrison
Printed and bound in Great Britain by Clays Ltd, Elcograf S.p.A.

For David

Contents

'… all my life, that thing about time passing. All my whole life long.'

– Marguerite Duras, *Practicalities*

'There seemed to be a disproportion in the whole thing, too big for me to do anything but grieve about.'

– Malachi Whitaker, *And So Did I*

'The world is white, we are lost, a great wind blows, and there in the background is a small black spot. We wonder what it is.'

– Hélène Cixous, *Three Steps on the Ladder of Writing*

Night Classes

'Are you coming, Ben?'

Emma was standing at the bottom of the stairs, watching her own fretful face in the mirror as she called up to their bedroom. Her face, she noticed, not for the first time, did not appear attractive when she opened her mouth wide; her chin sort of disappeared into her neck, made worse this evening by her scarf, already wound tight. She was getting hot, waiting in the hall.

'Ben?'

She was tempted to just go, but also knew that this would cause more trouble later. If he didn't emerge soon, she would have to go up. She pictured it, going up the stairs, him hearing the creak from the bed, the secret thrill he'd feel at having won, at having broken her. She saw herself opening the door, the lump of him, curled up under the covers with his back to her, or perhaps sitting on the edge, elbows on knees and hands together, looking down at his feet, waiting to be coaxed into conversation – waiting for her submission. Then what? She'd have to go to him, to kiss him, touch him, and let him slowly come round. She would then have to allow him to take off her gloves and scarf and coat, to prove that she was willing – no, *happy* – to stay there with him, because they loved each other and, to him, that would be the natural thing, the *right* thing, to do. Running through it in her mind, she also knew that she would then have to submit to sex, to let him pull her down, and to appear to want it, so as to soften the hurt she'd caused him; to partake, at the very least, in the symbolic gesture of the two of them, making love – making a baby.

Emma didn't want a baby. She'd told him so over dinner. She'd always said she wasn't sure, that she might never want one. And he'd said that was fine, he wasn't sure either, they could decide later. Now, they'd been married for four years; she was thirty-four, and Ben was thirty-six, and he'd said, over a low-sugar, gluten-free, vegetarian lasagne (which he'd cooked), that he thought she should stop taking the pill – that they should start trying for a baby. She'd laughed into her plate before answering. His tone had been so earnest, so assertive, betraying it as a rehearsed statement. When she did respond, sipping from her wine before she spoke, trying to keep it light, he'd been so shocked that he'd made a point of literally stopping eating. He'd put down his knife and fork, and stared at her. Soon after, he'd quietly professed himself not hungry (Emma's plate was almost empty, while he'd barely touched a thing), and taken himself to bed.

'Fuck this,' she muttered, watching as her cheeks reddened in the hall, feeling the sweat begin to crawl up her back. She didn't want to have to unparcel herself, she wanted to get going, to step out into the fresh, sharp cold, to walk briskly and listen to the evening sounds and watch her exhalations plume in bursts of white before disappearing into the surrounding air. She pulled at the front of her scarf uncomfortably. Whenever she got remotely too hot, she became convinced she was going to faint, although she'd never yet fainted in her life. She felt light-headed, and sick in her stomach.

Please come to the top of the stairs … Please, she thought. *If you would just come to the top of the stairs, if you would just come meet me in the middle, I'll consider staying. If you meet me halfway, we can talk about it, we can find a way.* She glanced from herself to the clock on the hall table – 19.48.

'Ben, honey, I'm going! It starts in ten minutes, I don't want to be late! … If you really don't want to come, that's fine, we can chat when I get home … or tomorrow!'

She'd paid for the class up front, had even called up the guy running it, Master Moshi, to make sure it really would be suitable for beginners. From the name, and the fact that it was karate, she'd thought he'd be Asian, but actually he was Irish too, from Donegal, his accent thick and untainted by Chicago.

'Aye yeah, it's suitable for everyone,' he'd said, 'and some of us usually go for a drink and a bit of a chat after, there's one o' those gammy Irish pubs on the corner there – I don't drink myself, but I go along for the craic … Sure, you can always come along and see how y'feel. Aye, your husband too, and is he Irish as well? Ah right, ah well sure, even so, the more the merrier – yep, yep, sound, see ya Thursday so!'

She knew nobody from home here. Her cousins had grown up here, and were all living in the suburbs. They had kids already, but whenever she spoke to them they seemed to just complain, about the children and their jobs, and talk about what they'd most recently binge-watched on Netflix. Their main issue with Emma was that, amongst their own friends and colleagues, they prided themselves on being Irish. This made them uneasy around her – she, who didn't speak 'Gaelic' or attend Irish Fests or play the fiddle or wear green t-shirts and *Guinness Is Good For You* baseball caps on Paddy's Day, but instead actually came from Ireland. They'd been close as kids, but all they had in common now was a penchant for heavy drinking, and that, she'd found, wasn't enough to carry a night out together, although it did get them through family weddings and Easter relatively painlessly.

Meanwhile, all of the friends she'd made through Ben and work were American – or, well, there was one French woman, who was married to a Canadian, and there was a Brazilian guy, and people with one or both parents from other countries, but they seemed to pride themselves on their ability to 'be' American; to belong here, in Chicago, in the land of opportunity. They talked about baseball and Trump and popular TV shows even more than the natives did, almost as though trying to prove the validity of their own presence. It was as if every outing was a test of their green card credentials. But they were all interesting, all amenable – so what was her problem? Ben often asked her this, saying she'd been quiet, even commenting that he'd caught her rolling her eyes once or twice.

She'd never managed to put it into words, but she felt now that what she missed was maybe something to do with being around people who understood themselves to be situated far from the centre of the world. She missed the feeling that came from being on a small island, with no more significance on a global scale than a toenail on a body. Although Ireland had been stifling when she lived there, from here, she remembered it feeling safe, easy, funny. She was sure there'd been less pomp, less earnestness, less *you-and-I-can-change-the-world*-ness. Although perhaps that had changed, and perhaps people were like this everywhere now. Certainly, her evenings out with Ben and his friends always began with sincere, heated discussions on gender or race issues, or congressional elections, and invariably ended up as a half tongue-in-cheek, half sincere debate amongst the born-and-bred Chicagoans about the heavily contested origins of blues music.

'Okay, sweetie, I'm going now, okay?' she watched herself flinch in the mirror as the word 'sweetie' forced its way from her lips – her use of it was in itself a peace offering, it being a term of endearment he favoured, but which she softly despised. No sound from upstairs though, nothing.

Fuckity fuckity fuckit anyway ... she thought. She made a point of pulling on her boots noisily, banging them around a bit and hooshing herself down onto the second step to tie them, her coat rustling with the activity. All the time, she was listening out for him – still nothing. No movement. He was holding firm. Her stomach constricted. She began to hum a Bill Withers tune, knowing he'd be straining to hear every little thing, wanting him to understand that, as far as she was concerned, this was not a cause for concern – she wanted him to believe that, to her, this was all easy, all casual. No big deal.

Emma's mother hadn't wanted her to marry Ben. She'd never said it expressly, was never anything but courteous towards him, but Emma knew. Emma could tell. Even on their wedding day, back in Ireland, her mother had been going through the motions – *getting through it.* Her father had bawled his eyes out, had given Ben a big bear hug the moment the ceremony was over, had kept going on and on to all of Ben's American relatives who'd come over about how happy he was for 'my beautiful little girl', how Ben was 'such a gentleman, such a good fella', and how they 'couldn't be happier' to have him in the family. He'd called them 'the Yanks' to their faces, gormlessly, and had bought them all pints of Guinness, which naturally they'd adored. Ben's younger cousins from South Carolina had even asked to get their photos taken with him, and had put little videos of him pretending to do a jig, elbows out and eyes half closed, on their TikToks: 'real irish dad @ wedding OMG!!'

But maybe her father had sensed it too, her mother's formality, and was overcompensating, Emma thought now. Her mother had acted properly, had worn new navy blue shoes and a new duck-egg blue dress, with matching short jacket and hat. She'd had her hair done, worn her good Clarins lipstick and her best pearls, had shaken hands and made conversation and smiled for the photos. But that was it. There had been a wall, a barrier, filled with all the unspoken things; her dreams for what Emma would become, an independent woman, travelling the world, an artist, liberated, wild even; all the things she herself would've liked to be, had she not fallen pregnant at nineteen. Instead, Emma was on her way to becoming a lawyer's wife in Chicago. A lawyer who made supposedly ironic jokes about leprechauns, and who talked openly and with relish about house prices and income thresholds and timely investments, and who'd teared up while reciting 'Scaffolding' by Seamus Heaney at the engagement party (seemingly the first Heaney poem he could find online that seemed to fit the occasion, although in truth, of course, it didn't fit at all). Emma's mind flinched from the humiliation of the memory.

She secretly wished, not for the first time, that her mother was here right now, to call his bullshit. Without her mother's guidance, Emma found it difficult, with Ben, to distinguish genuine grievances from manipulation. She couldn't tell, even now, whether there was actually any bullshit to call. Was this sulking in bed completely justified? Should she be the one saying sorry?

Whenever Emma suspected he was being unfair, or petulant, or mean, he was able to explain to her, slowly and patiently, how she was in fact – if she could only look at the situation properly, unclouded by her emotions – completely wrong. How, *in truth*, she was the one being stubborn, or pig-headed, or cruel. He had shown her, more than once, how she weaponized their respective genders against him, making it seem as though he was playing the role of the 'unkind husband', when really all he ever wanted was to be with her and get along with her and live their lives happily ever after. She wasn't stupid, she knew about gaslighting, about the subtle bullying that can happen within a relationship. The difference, she felt, was that Ben really did love her, and he did seem to only want what he felt was best for the both of them – he sincerely wanted to be with her, to spend his entire life with her, and for each of them to be given the opportunity to better themselves through their relationship. He took her criticisms seriously. He had stopped whistling around the house when she'd asked him to, and had diligently worked on his technique when giving head, even signing up to a men's website that offered useful tips. He'd gone on to buy a recommended ebook about keeping their sex life both stimulating and loving, written by some legendary Peruvian-American sex therapist with a PhD and a podcast.

Yet, in spite of all this dedication, all of this 'constructive growth', he never seemed to do enough for her. He told her that it made him more sad than anything else in the world that she never seemed fully satisfied. Emma tried to reassure him that she was happy, as happy as she possibly could be. But even so, and although he'd never said it directly, Emma had come to understand from their marriage that she was an exceptionally cold person. Cold and perhaps even quite selfish. When she voiced this fear to him, he said, 'how could you not have some issues around happiness and satisfaction, with a mother like that?' He then went on to tell her that he loved her, and would always love her, in spite of her flaws.

So maybe he was right, to be so upset? And maybe, as she'd always suspected, there was something seriously wrong with her, for not wanting children.

This question, openly thought, made Emma feel for a moment as though she might actually throw up. Laces tied, she sat still on the stairs, doubled over into her thick coat, considering. Had she misled him, about having kids? Was it a given that she was eventually supposed to want them? Were all women supposed, in the end, to want them? But she didn't. She pictured one, a little mewling baby; waking in the night to feed it, never free of it, always tied to it, never able to just get up and go and walk out, or to take a train somewhere, to be free. Not that she did that much anyway, took trains to places unexpectedly (in fact, she never did), but with a baby, the option would be gone – gone for *ever*. Emma treasured the idea of her freedom, even if she never actually made any use of it. It was like a gemstone, hidden away in her pocket, unseen, but there for her to touch, to stroke, whenever she felt like it.

Maybe this was just more proof of her selfishness, this need to keep her options open. She had married Ben, but that, she knew deep down, was less *definitely* permanent than a baby. She could, if she absolutely had to, leave a husband, but she wouldn't be able to leave a baby. Not that she intended to leave Ben. Emma believed in the commitment of marriage, believed in making it work. Her parents had been through terrible times, her father's drinking, the infidelities, the roaring fights, but they'd always come through. And now they were about as happy as a couple their age could be, she reckoned. They'd be lost without one another, at least. And that was something.

Part of the attraction, for Emma, had been this sense of permanence, and the introduction of boundaries. Of limits. She had been brought up in a whirlwind of possibilities. All her life, her mother had insisted that she could be anyone, do anything, go anywhere. That, in fact, she was obliged to be exceptional. When, out for lunch years ago, Emma's father's sister had suggested she would make a wonderful teacher, her mother had been so offended that they'd left. Everywhere she'd looked, the future stretched out into distant horizons with no discernible ends. All of this had, for Emma, morphed into a strange, even crippling, burden – she developed a kind of future-phobia, faced so mercilessly with all the hope poured into her by her mother, her culture, her position as middle class, intelligent, healthy, capable. A husband with needs and expectations, a particular place to live, a commitment of some kind, anchored Emma. It provided her with an outline, a life shape, *within* which she had hoped she would be, if anything, more free.

Still, in spite of all the warnings about how difficult marriage is, offered by women's magazines and most of Emma's unhappy female relatives, it had proved more difficult than she'd imagined. Knowing it to be reversible, knowing herself to still hold the *possibility* of total freedom, had helped her to cope with the tight strictures of her days. Cleaning, grocery shopping, keeping fit, keeping busy, seeing people, not to mention her work as an assistant to one of Chicago's top corporate photographers – all of it was okay because, ultimately, if she needed to, she could up and leave. When she thought this logic out to its end, it made her feel uncomfortable. Maybe she had never really committed fully to her marriage? Maybe the coldness Ben accused her of was actually something clinical, or a sign of something deeper, something unfixable and immovable within her. *Oh God, probably,* she thought, squeezing closed her eyes for a moment.

Emma untied her boots, and then, annoyed at herself, at the whole situation, she tied them again, tighter. She stood up. What to do? She saw herself in the mirror, and caught, before she could adjust it, her worried, tired expression. She spent an inordinate amount of time reminding herself to unfurrow her brow, and was always unconsciously running her fingers between her eyebrows, to smooth out the deep groove that was forming there. Recently, in the evenings, watching movies with Ben, she'd found herself half scrolling through her phone, researching options for filler and Botox treatments. She didn't think she'd ever really do it, although when she had casually mentioned the idea to Ben, he'd pulled her in for an earnest hug and said, 'you should do whatever makes you happy, sweetie – we have the money.'

Catching herself, she looked, in that moment, older – finally looked her age, perhaps. In spite of her incoming forehead wrinkle, people always told her she looked young. Most people guessed she was somewhere between twenty-six and twenty-nine. Her skin had always been bright and firm, like her mother's. But now she was thirty-four. *Thirty-four.* How had that happened?

*

They'd started dating when she was twenty-eight. At that point, she'd had a string of crappy boyfriends, her photography was going nowhere, she was living back at home. In spite of all those gaping opportunities, those hand-wringing expectations, she'd been sinking into failure. And then along came Ben. A Tinder date, in Dublin for the night. *Why not?* she'd thought, sitting in the lunchroom of the office where she was temping. Wealthy, charming, American. It'd be an experience, at the very least. He'd picked up the 'cheque', after which she'd felt obliged to sleep with him. The next morning, he'd offered to extend his stay by another week. 'Why don't we just see where this goes? Give it a chance?' he'd said, staring into her eyes and touching her hair in the hotel bed. His eyes were big and blue and lined with thick black lashes. It was like he was playing a part in a cheesy film, but it was a film she kind of liked, in spite of herself. He was so shamelessly *Hollywood*, with his white teeth and expensive-looking plain t-shirts and embarrassing texts – 'hey Ems, I just want you to know that you are one in a million <3'. It was ridiculous, but also refreshing. He fucked her every which way, but insisted, after the first drunken night, that they always be face to face when one or the other of them came. He wanted them to come together, and felt so strongly about it, about what it would mean for them, for their 'fledgling love', that she started faking, just to appease him. The first time he believed they'd come together, staring at one another, his eyes welled up with emotion. Then he'd buried his face in her hair, coyly pretending he didn't want her to see how moved he was. It was sweet, she'd thought, stroking his back – romantic. Yes, a little ridiculous, but also, yes, definitely romantic.

The Irish guy she'd been with before Ben had usually arrived around 9 p.m. with a Chinese takeaway in a plastic bag and a few cans for himself. He'd played video games on her housemate's Xbox while she sat beside him on her phone, and then they'd go upstairs so he could fuck her from behind and come on her back. He'd never once stayed over, claiming to only sleep well in his own bed. So whatever else Ben had been, he was, she told herself again, staring into the mirror, without question, an enormous improvement.

He'd been the one to suggest she move in with him, just three months later. 'You'd like Chicago, it's too hot, then it's too cold, and the whole time it's *super* violent – good for photos, right?' he'd said, laughing over Skype. She'd been to Chicago many times as a child, had gone with her parents to visit the family there, but Ben had always spoken of it as though she hadn't. He just sort of blocked out the fact of her already knowing it, probably because he wanted to be the one to give it to her. He kept saying he couldn't wait to show her around – he was the first person she'd ever met who actually referred to it as 'the Windy City!' He told her he'd take her out on the town, introduce her to everyone, maybe even throw a party. She'd told herself that this, too, was charming. Low on other viable options, and sick of her mother's expectant silences, she'd moved over immediately, booking the flights before she had time to think herself out of it.

And, to be fair to him, he'd done it all, and more. There was no denying that he'd held up his end. Even now, after all these years, she felt indebted to him. His apartment then had been beautiful, as was this house, which they'd bought a year later (with his family money, although he'd insisted on putting it in both their names). He'd encouraged her to decorate it however she liked, to buy all new furniture, anything. Emma had never been especially interested in interior design, but was touched by his faith, and threw herself into it. They'd painted the walls together, in all the colours she'd carefully chosen. Pale blue, mossy green, oxblood red. Every time they opened a new pot for another room, he marvelled: 'Wow! Oh my God, it's beautiful, wow, so beautiful sweetie, what a great choice!'

Ben was invariably attentive and exceptionally kind. When she'd first arrived, and went for all those job interviews at magazines, or tried to pimp out her photographs as a freelancer to newspapers, he'd supported her, believed in her, cooked comforting and nutritious meals for her. Whenever she was upset or had cramps, he ran frothy, scented baths for her. He bought her lots of little gifts, perfumes and lingerie, but he respected her opinions too, listened to her, watched the films and read the books she recommended, so that they could talk about them together. *This Wuthering Heights, it's crazy, holy crap!!! Loving it, xxxxx,* he'd texted from his morning commuter train. He wanted to devour everything she could offer him, and told her that he wanted to give her back all he had in return. He taught her, without ever acknowledging it overtly, that this was how love worked – an equitable sharing out of what you had. She realized she'd never known this before, perhaps because she'd never met a man remotely interested in what she had to offer.

It used to be the case that a night class like this would be more his thing than hers – she'd always hated group activities, until he'd shown her how much she needed to lighten up.

'Not everyone's an idiot, Emma. You gotta give other human beings a chance, y'know?' And although, mostly, they did prove to be idiots, he was right – some were okay. And it was nice to be among them, regardless, even if only to feel smug and superior at times. Ben had taught her the importance of regular human contact for maintaining her mood. Besides anything else, the busyness meant she had less time to overthink, and thus be anxious, or wallow.

Now, she did a pottery class on Monday evenings, a knitting class every second Tuesday, Zumba on Fridays and spinning on Saturday mornings, while he went to the gym on Mondays and Tuesdays, did yoga on Wednesday mornings before work, and played baseball with friends in a local league most Sundays in the season. And, right now, this very moment, they were both supposed to be starting eight weeks of Thursday night karate, with the option to extend.

'Sweetheart?'

With tension sending electric currents up her hot, sticky back, she waited for a response. Nothing. This wasn't how she always looked, surely? It must be the hall light, she decided; even her blonde hair appeared ashy and grey. The more she stared at herself, the less her face seemed like her own. She suddenly wished she had her camera to hand, to capture this moment.

Then she remembered that she used to do this all the time – take self-portraits. Herself at her worst, her most raw, when she'd been crying in her room for days, or when she was agonizingly hungover. She'd created an anti-Instagram account, called herself 'Meme-a O'Deatherty' instead of Emma O'Doherty, and filled it with the most awful, revoltingly honest selfies; of puss-filled, yellow spots on her face, or her own boozy puke in the loo, or strange, hard-to-discern images of the rolls of fat on her belly when she leaned forward, taken so close up that they looked like the patterns made by the tide on a pink sandy beach, or an unfinished Georgia O'Keeffe landscape. The whole project had been no more than a poor imitation of other women's work, that of Francesca Woodman or Cindy Sherman or Nan Goldin, only without any of the waiflike elegance or fascination or deep, implicit meanings. Yet, there'd been something in it, a green shoot of a concept, if only she'd had the courage to not give up, to not lose faith in her ideas. Not to cower in shame at the mere thought that she, too, was allowed to have, never mind try to express, those ideas.

How had she forgotten all that, she wondered? And why, she now tried to recall, had she done it? She vaguely remembered she'd thought it really was terribly meaningful, that she was making some sort of artistic statement, something about lies, narratives, lived truth. All the usual 'I'm-in-my-twenties-and-I-still-have-ideals' notions, no doubt. The thought made her strangely sad. So sad that, for a moment, she felt like crying.

Meme-a O'Deatherty had only had around thirty-seven followers, and most of those were either bots or her relatives. And still, remembering it so sharply – the very fact of remembering at all, highlighted to her all of the things about her younger self she might still be forgetting, the things she might for ever, now, forget – made her feel as if she had lost something, something irrevocable. It came to her, however fleetingly, as an acute and poignant grief.

Thinking about it now, standing silently in the hallway of her married home, in America, so far away from that time, from that place, miles and miles of land and ocean and years already spent, Emma heard without registering the sound of someone walking by on the pavement outside, and wheels, pushing something, a buggy maybe. A car passed, then another. Someone nearby was trying to parallel park, through the closed door came the engine shifting gears back and forth, the squeak of tyre against pavement. In the distance, a siren. The house, silent too, hummed. Was this how she was going to live the rest of her life? Was this how she'd see it out? She glanced at the clock – 19.53.

'Right!' she sighed loudly.

'Cunting fucking fuck this …' she muttered, frustrated, but also trying to pump herself up, to convert her grief and fear and weariness into rage, the way she'd often seen her father do when her mother had upset him. He'd never been one to cry, he'd get angry. It was the same with her mother, actually, although her anger had been silent, treacherous – the black hole anger of quietly closed doors and pursed lips, rather than that helpless raging outward of her father. Her mother's style had, of course, invariably proved more deadly.

'Fucking selfish cunt pussy *dick* …' she said, a little louder this time, shoving away the rising uneasiness, picking up her backpack, retrieving her keys from the bowl. Now, decision made, rage growing freely, expanding out from her stomach like a mushroom cloud unfurling in slow motion, she moved swiftly, forcefully, keen to get out, to get free of that toxic heavy lovesick air as quickly as she could. She jerked open the front door, felt the *whoosh* of cold hit her hot cheeks, and smiled.

'Fucking wanking cunty cockface *bastard*!' she announced into the night.

'Bye then!' she called over her shoulder, almost giddy now, almost laughing in the delightfully surging hate she was allowing herself to feel for him, for this, for everything. *Fuck the house, fuck the street, fuck the night, fuck the air, fuck Chicago, fuck everything that this living is turning out to be! Fuck it all, and then fuck it again for good measure! Leave no stone unfucked!*

She would go to the night class, fuck it, why not? She'd work up a sweat, chat to people, chew the ear off them, be her most charming fuckity-fuckit self, and then she'd go out and get wasted, totally fucking wasted, like she hadn't been for years! Through her mind flashed an image of Ben's loving face – his face from the early days, that seemed always to be mouthing the words 'I adore you' in her memory – and in that moment, for the first time, she felt no love at all.

'Fuck him!' she almost shouted, smiling. She felt, just then, how school shooters must feel – elated on pain, *high* on hate. She stepped outside. She may have heard something from upstairs, some movement, a light step perhaps, or the creaking of a door, but she chose not to register.

Ah, that cold, sharp air! The same air swirling all the way from here, this very moment, all across the world – across deserts, seas, cities, fields, rivers, forests, fishing villages, sandy beaches and glacial plains, on and on for ever; across all the bodies, the eyes and breasts and smalls of backs, the knees and shoulders and cocks and pussies of the world, the sweat-slicked skins and soft-to-the-touch lips, and they were all hers, too, if she wanted them. She was still young enough, could still be free, and she understood in this moment that she would be, soon, again – she could fucking *feel* it.

Let's Dance

On the night of Joe's birthday, Kate arrived late, cheap bottle of Pinot Grigio in hand, and a card containing a €10 book voucher, since Joe used to love reading, but now loved to say, mournfully, that he could 'never seem to find the time'. Yet, in spite of not reading (instead, dedicating his free time to podcasts and popular TV series on the various streaming platforms), he still liked to be thought of as a 'reading type', and so he thanked her wholeheartedly, with a hug, even though she hated hugging, as he was well aware:

'Ah, Kate, you shouldn't have – thanks!'

The meal was a Middle Eastern vegan mezze, made by Maria, with not nearly enough for everyone to feel sated, followed by an equally small fruit salad with organic coconut yoghurt, presented in a kooky bowl from Zara Home. Once it was finished, after offering to help clean up (an offer Maria always politely but firmly refused, ever since Kate had dropped and smashed one of her grandmother's plates, one of the six salvaged from the old family farm in Toledo), Kate rose from the table and, taking her glass, sat back down in her usual spot, feet tucked under her, at the far end of the rental-property leather couch in Joe and Maria's Dublin 8 two-bed. Soon, she was joined by Tom and Pete, who sat in their usual seats to her left and, after a little while, Joe and Maria, who always sat across from and beside her, respectively.

'I know man, I know …' said Tom, who was incredibly muscly and came from a farming family in Laois, as he took the proffered place mat of coke from Pete who, fairly muscly and from Texas, was rubbing the remains of his line into his gums, wide-eyed.

'… and like, obviously I don't eat meat, or, well like, barely ever –'

Here, Maria tried to cut in with an admonishment against *ever daring* to eat those poor, beautiful creatures, but Tom, knowing this was going to happen – even when not high, Maria never fucking stopped – raised his voice slightly and continued speaking over her, '– only, like, if I'm in a fancy steak restaurant with my dad or something, y'know? Or at a barbecue, or in France or whatever …'

Joe, sipping his beer, nodded in understanding from his armchair, already a bit drunk and high. Maria, sitting across from Joe, on the sofa beside Kate, glared at him pointedly for even tacitly agreeing.

'… and I drink soya milk, or almond, or whatever's going, like, other than cow, of course,' continued Tom loudly over a Stevie Wonder track.

'Dude,' Pete cut in, decisively and with grave seriousness, as though his life, nay, all their lives, depended on it; 'oat is the only way to go, it's the only –'

Tom tried to cut back in here, nodding effusively to show he knew this already, that he hadn't meant to admit to drinking any other variety, but Pete was on a victorious roll and it was more difficult, of course, to talk over Pete. This was because men's points were, Kate thought, knocking back her fourth – or was it fifth? – glass of bitter white wine and already craving her next one, harder to ignore outright than women's (seeing as, whatever about their self-professed feminism, men still considered one another their *actual* equals):

'... 'cause, like, think about it,' Pete went on, shaking his head slightly for emphasis, 'almond milk is causing all those droughts in California, right? Which is causing all the wildfires –'

'– Oh *God*, did you guys see the little burnt koala today? His little *ears*!?' said Maria, almost crying at the mere memory, her display of womanly empathy (which became more pronounced when she'd been drinking) overcoming her as she reached for her phone, to find it now, again, and show them all.

'That's Australia, love,' said Joe.

'I *know*, Joe, jeesh! Still, is all connected, righ'?'

'– and soya milk is causing, like, major deforestation in the rainforest,' Pete continued, also resolutely ignoring Maria's interjections, 'you must know that, *right*?'

Finishing his point, Kate observed that Pete had become even more wide-eyed, overcome by the terrible truth he had spoken unto the rest of them, or perhaps by a rush of cocaine hitting his bloodstream. Pointedly, he stared into the eyes of each of them, one by one. Tom, refusing to meet his gaze, irritated, sat perched and frowning on the footstool to Pete's left, directly in front of the TV. Because of the low height of the seat, his thick, gym-hewn thigh muscles were forced into a semi-perch, causing the stitches along the seams of his chinos to unwillingly expand. Kate couldn't take her eyes from a little dusting of white caught in the hair of his moustache just below his left nostril. She despaired at the waste of it, and wanted to get up, walk over, and lick it off him. Pete, after circling the room with his eyes, gazed at him with an intensely concerned expression, as though the future of the planet rested on Tom's digesting what he'd just said. Pete, who was gangly and blonde and wide-jawed, without being remotely handsome, perhaps due to his tiny button nose and squinty, Matt Damon-style eyes, was actually beginning to lean, almost imperceptibly, further and further towards Tom, like Oprah subtly leaning into an interviewee to add a sense of intimacy as well as drama, trying (with *nothing* but love and empathy) to dig out the juicy bits from, say, a divorced celebrity, or a victim of sexual abuse.

These other guests were friends of Joe's from work. Predictably, all three were employed in an American technology firm that had originally chosen Dublin as its European headquarters for the tax breaks (or, more plainly, to avoid paying appropriate amounts of tax). Everyone who worked for these companies had always known about this, and scoffed at how awful it was, but no one ever seemed to take a harder stance on the immorality of it than a short, terse shake of the head followed by a shrug.

This was because they ultimately saw taxes as money that the government stupidly and ineffectually disappeared into nothing and nowhere, to mend roads that didn't need mending, or to put towards private holidays for themselves or into fat cats' pockets, or to fund useless artists painting their own belly buttons and calling it art, or to build yet another ugly, unwanted housing estate in the midlands. Or, even worse, they vaguely believed – the belief would not retain its shape if pressed, but never being articulated openly, it was never pressed – that their hard-earned money was used to support those people who were too lazy or stupid or fat or addicted to support themselves.

This belief was in no way connected to the marches they went on to fight for the rights of the disenfranchised. The disenfranchised were somehow different to these people snuffling up their taxes, these pigs they saw languishing about on benefits, greedily consuming all the state could give them and belching out nothing in return. They cared about the worthy poor, they truly wanted *their* lives to get better. Yet sometimes, walking past a stinking mess of flattened boxes in a doorway in Dublin, or hearing some skinny, stumbling person with their top lip pierced hollering at another down an otherwise civilized street, or observing an addict on their cramped DART ride home, sleeping across two whole seats, filthily oblivious to everyone else, they couldn't help thinking that, yes, although of course there were a few genuinely sad cases worth helping, a few people who really were simply unlucky and in need (cute children, for example, and their unfortunate young mothers – well, the ones who'd never gotten into drugs), that these were the exceptions.

Mostly though, the state was funding the ugly, sordid lifestyles of the unappealing majority, those people who, in other times, would have been called the plebeians, or the peasantry. All those people who just didn't have any *self-control*, any discipline. Those who clearly didn't know how to work, or didn't want to. God, what they'd give, these guys, to sit around on their arses all day, not having to go to work, and instead receive money for doing nothing. They were all for benefits, but surely there needed to be stricter rules for those who received them? Did these people *really* need them, and for how long? You'd think that they'd at least do something with the free time, to better themselves: get clean, or get fit, or get some education, or, like, write a fucking novel. The least they could do was stop having children, forever adding to the problem. Ah, but with more children, they got more benefits, were moved up the housing lists, they thought ruefully. Although, as aforementioned, they'd never openly admit, even to themselves, to the existence of these thoughts, being, as a rule, progressive, left-leaning, forward-thinking, totally inclusive liberals. And so, if corporate tax-dodging was, in essence, stealing from the poor to feed the rich, at least it was only stealing from the *unworthy* poor, to feed the *worthy* rich, like them and their bosses.

Besides, these American firms treated them, the employees, very well. They had ping-pong tables in the rec room, and free craft beers in the fridge in the Scandi-style canteen area (although no one ever actually drank the beers, unless it was a Friday evening brainstorming sesh, one that had yet again run beyond official work hours, and their direct superior had firmly encouraged them to do so). There was even a gym, which most employees attended at least once a day, so as to be seen there and to keep up with everyone else. Also, they went to the gym to clear their minds, or at least, that's what they were *told* they ought to be using it for by their superiors in the weekly Employee Health & Welfare emails. All they wanted, these emails proclaimed, was a happy and healthy workforce who felt positive about coming into work – and mostly they *did* enjoy coming in, they reckoned, even though they had to arrive early most days and work late most nights, and even though they had performance reviews every two months, and the competition to remain in employment was cut-throat, causing burnout among many (relegating them to the pile of the 'too weak' or 'too dumb' or 'just not cut out for life in the fast lane').

They bragged about it, in fact, how cool it was to work there, and the endurance it required to succeed – almost like how Kate imagined army dudes would brag in some dive bar about doing a tour in Iraq or Afghanistan. Although Joe, Pete and Tom did admit, with wry smiles, that they only put up with it all because of their insanely generous pay package and the regular opportunities for bonuses (based on those bimonthly performance reviews). If it wasn't for the money, they'd be off doing other things, most likely dabbling in the arts – Pete fancied himself a visual artist; Tom, a musician; and Joe, of course, a poet. But those jobs wouldn't pay the bills, they reasoned, nor for the holidays abroad, nor for the iPhones or gig tickets, or meals out, nor – and this was fair enough – the copious amounts of cocaine and ketamine and MDMA and ecstasy and booze that they consumed at weekends, largely to counteract the dread of the oncoming week, in which they'd earn all that money again, to again buy drugs to make the prospect of the week after that bearable – and so forth.

Joe was naturally slim, and preferred to run to and from work than spend time in the gym (after all, he now had a girlfriend and a baby to get home to), but Pete and Tom were buff – especially Tom, who was pinkly ginger, and wore slim-fit t-shirts that looked like any moment they might tear, Hulk-style, from the pressure of his bulging, veiny arm muscles which, Kate suspected, he flexed even while sitting still. More than once, he had noticed her staring at the sharp, white knuckles of his fists, and had actively made a point of stretching out his fingers and placing them on the table or on his thighs, or picking up a drink, embarrassed to have been caught clenching when he ought to have been relaxing. All of this, Kate assumed, he did to make up for his own hang-ups about being short but, to Kate, it made him look taut and veiny, rather than strong. On the rare occasion that her mind wandered to the image of Tom, she always pictured a slightly nervous English bulldog, eyes distrustful and jaw set, alert to imagined ridicule or threat, forever straining forward against its harness.

This night, feeling light and unanchored from the meagre dinner (but not caring especially, because of the drugs, which dissipated any hunger), Kate sat just as she had sat on many occasions over the last two years or so, doing lines of coke from the same old tomato sauce-stained place mat, the music from one of Joe's Spotify playlists kneading and stretching the thick silence all around them; that awful, omniscient silence, forever ready to come in and burst their illusion of happy, easy camaraderie. They had been discussing the environment again. They always came back, one way or the other, to discussing the environment, how everything was fucked.

'Yeah, but like, if we're gonna be realistic about it, it's already too late, y'know? Like all this tree planting and that, it's all just, like, a placebo thing, y'know, to soothe the masses, like how they put buttons on the pedestrian crossings in Dublin – it's just to give us the illusion of control, that we're actually doing something …'

'What d'ya mean?'

'I mean, like, no matter what we do now, the world is going to die anyway, it's too late, we –'

'No, no, I know that, I mean about the crosswalks in Dublin.'

'Oh, yeah man, the buttons, for the green man? They don't do anything, they're all on a timer – it's just to calm people, so they know, like, their turn is coming.'

'There's one real one.'

'Oh yeah?'

'That's crazy!'

'Yeah, outside the government building, eh, Leinster House, is it? On Kildare Street.'

'This is crazy.'

'Fuckin' typical.'

'I know, right?'

'Like they're the only bastards in an actual hurry.'

'Fuckin' democracy, my arse.'

'Ha! Dude, yes! Crazy ...'

Here, Maria interjected, sitting forward on the couch, her big, brown eyes filled with fright: 'But, Tom, do you really think dere's no hope? I mean, whad about the children, the next generation, whass gonna happen to them? To my Marta?'

She sounded genuinely terrified, but then, she had just snorted her line, and the sharp intensity of emotion had probably been caused by the sudden rush of coke into her system. Also, Kate thought, she loved being dramatic, uber-feminine, all love and concern and *but think of the children*-y. Tom didn't answer, was unable to, and the ensuing pause in conversation was thankfully somewhat covered by the soothing, undulating tones of Hiatus Kaiyote. Reaching out in a sudden jerking motion for his beer bottle, Joe knocked it over, causing a heavy clank, white foam tumbling in spasms from its still-shuddering neck. A split-second later, only just too late to be convincingly believable, Maria jumped theatrically, throwing her hands to her chest and exclaiming in giggling fright: 'Joe! Ah! Whad are you doing!'

In the moment of shocked silence that followed, there ran, through all of their minds, as there always did on these nights, with no need to say anything aloud, flashing images of polar bears swimming out to nowhere, lost and starving from lack of ice; thin brown people with flooded hut-like houses, stoical or wailing, always holding dirty and thin yet impossibly cherubic children; more floods; landslides; mass graves; orange-glowing, smoke-strewn skies from wildfires burning out of control; and, finally, flitting in a perfectly synchronized formation across the surfaces of each of their five brains, that *Planet Earth* footage of the sloth, lost and frightened, smiling benignly as it's carried out of a post-apocalyptic, ashen and treeless section of what was, for generations, its habitat in the rainforest – that ancient homeland gone now, chopped to smithereens to make paper for receipts and parking tickets and immediately discarded shopping or to-do lists …

And to think, it was *all their fault all their fault all their fault.*

Where was that cocaine, Kate thought – *ah, here it is, my turn!*

Sniffff … snifffff … ah, yes, all gone now, mind clean white, singing electric, yes.

Wiping her nostrils with thumb and forefinger, before handing the place mat along, Kate observed that the consensus seemed to be that if you were one of those people simply enjoying your life, finding any comfort within it, rather than constantly suffering from a series of strict, self-imposed deprivations, terrified of all the harm you were causing, every second of every day, then it was even more your fault, because you were fucking ignorant too. That was the cost of living now, as a good conscientious person who deserved their place on the planet – the careful maintenance of an unrelenting, crippling awareness of the pain and degradation your life was causing others.

And it was simultaneously your duty to remain forever distracted, through activities, purchases, social media and getting resoundingly fucked up, as they were here tonight. Both at once, on and on for ever until whichever died first: you or the planet.

This experience of life as they were now obliged to live it felt, at times, unbearable. It was a crushing pressure, and there was no way to redeem it, no truly effective way to relieve oneself of one's part in the Earth's destruction. People ran marathons, had kids, wrote books, worked themselves to the bone, toned their stomachs, went to Ibiza, planted trees, knitted, learned to cook burnt Basque cheesecakes, not because they really wanted to, but because, in truth, these things were all that was left to them, these placebos, these routes to partial oblivion. They were ways of keeping one's eyes lowered. And yes, this night, sitting here, was one of those methods, but as always, they ended up just talking about it all anyway, how they were doomed, and how they were culpable, how it was all their fault.

A phone was thrust into Kate's line of vision from her right. On the screen, a badly burnt koala, his ears all frayed and bloody and steaming, his little clinging body covered in black and red-raw patches.

'See?' Maria asked, staring into Kate's face, her pupils dilated so widely that her dark brown corneas looked totally obscured, giving her a sort of pretty teen-vampire quality. *Why isn't she blinking?* wondered Kate nervously, shifting in her seat, trying not to see the image of the koala, all small and sad and confused and burning, which was all her fault, because she drove places in a car and sometimes ordered chicken curry or a burger from Deliveroo. She didn't want to see, hated all this, this grief porn, this self-lacerating guilt-mongering that people of her generation always ended up indulging in. What difference did it make anyway, these stupid conversations? *None none none.*

She considered asking Maria if she wanted to dance, but immediately thought better of it. She'd hate to give Maria the opportunity to start into all her faux-Latina hip swaying and sashaying about. Kate felt her heart rate rising, a sudden sensation of there not being quite enough air to go round, not quite enough space in the room. She gripped the cool, leathery arm of the sofa, and forced herself to breathe, slowly. Where was that cocaine now? How long had it –? Ah, it was with Pete, he was topping it up, then around again, through Tom, Joe and Maria, and back to her, not far – Tom was already having his go now, that was quick, actually, wasn't it? That would sort her out, maybe. To her left, Maria, who was still pretending to feel tearful about the koala, was now looking up photos and videos of other burnt animals who'd been caught up in wildfires, and gasping at each one to fuel her own sorrow.

In Kate's mind, Maria was one of those people who believed the entire happenings of the world around her were a series of support acts, upon all of which she must pass judgement, or to all of which she must react. This was the Maria show, it all was, *reality*, the entire functioning of the world, whether the rest of them liked it or not – although she assumed, of course, that they not only liked it, but *loved* it. It was all a means for discovering more about Maria, the incredible, magnificent gift that was the birth and existence of Maria. Maria, the ultimate individual, who was PA to the assistant manager in a start-up company that made natural beauty products which sold for insanely high prices. Maria, who'd studied marketing at university in Madrid. Maria, from Ciudad Real, who now lived in Dublin with her beautiful little baby girl and the love of her life, Joe, from Cavan, who in turn worked in IT at a big tech firm. The one and only, the exceptionally impressive, unspeakably special Maria, for whom they were all here tonight, their primary roles in life being solely to assist in opening up the genius and potential of Maria, Maria, *Mariaaaa*!

They were her chorus, her extras, her backing singers – Maria! Wise Millennial, Feminist, Benevolent Queen of the Earth, Mother of God (if you believed in that sort of thing, which of course Maria didn't) – Maria! And this impression she gave Kate, of being the star of her own reality TV show, only got worse when Maria did coke (naturally enough). Alongside all of this, needless to say, was Maria's self-professed low self-esteem and crippling anxiety, for which she was seeing a therapist, and that meant, along with the necessity of their worshipping her, they had to be extremely aware of her feelings, and how small, seemingly harmless comments or looks might negatively affect her – which again, as though by magic, made it all about Maria.

'How's the writing going?'

Kate heard this coming towards her from the left, Pete's direction, and so swivelled her body sharply back to her right, Maria's way. Immediately, Maria began shoving the phone into her face again, whose screen now displayed an image of a sizzled but still just-about-alive baby kangaroo being pulled from its dead mother's pouch.

'I don't want to see that,' Kate muttered, clamping her eyes shut, although still not turning back towards Pete (even these sizzled baby animals were preferable to talking about her non-existent writing). But Maria pretended not to hear her, and kept forcing the images on her, as though they were some kind of evidence.

'What's that?' asked Joe, who was intimately familiar with Maria's desire for constant attention, and who pandered to this demand because, for him, it was easier that way. Immediately, Maria lifted the phone from Kate's face, and raised it aloft to show Joe and the rest of the room, sighing in aching sympathy as she did so and putting her head to one side, to convey how moving *she especially* found the images. Pete and Tom looked at the screen, grimaced, and shook their heads just fractionally in an appropriate show of masculine sorrow.

'Ah,' said Joe mournfully, looking openly heartbroken, his eyes almost welling (though not quite). He could afford to be a little more feminine because he lived with his girlfriend and the child they'd made together.

Suddenly, they all noticed that Maria and Joe's baby had been crying in the other room for a while.

'Oh, that's what that noise is!' laughed Pete, before realizing his mistake and quickly changing his face, unconvincingly, to an expression of concern.

Maria leapt up to attend to her daughter, throwing Joe a filthy look as she did so. Joe, under her angry instruction, turned down the music slightly, although experience told them all that it would go back up, once they comfortably forgot about the baby again.

'How is Marta?' Pete asked politely, his jaw gurning.

'She's amazing man, amazing. Seriously ...'

'Ah, cool man.'

'Yeah, that's so deadly,' said Tom, not smiling or looking up, but rather tidying his line before leaning over to snort it up. He furrowed his brow and breathed in sharply through his nostrils as he sat up again. 'And, uh, she's not a year yet, right?'

'She's thirteen months and six days,' said Joe, smiling dreamily, before asking, 'do you want to see some pictures?' and reaching into his pocket.

'Sure, I can see the montage there,' said Tom, deflecting Joe's phone by pointing to the photos stuck over one another in a large glass frame that hung behind the couch, above Kate's head. All three of the men looked at the wall, their eyes not quite focused, to admire.

'*Collage*,' Kate muttered. She too could have strained around to look, but didn't bother.

'She's beautiful, man,' said Pete, still gurning.

'Yeah, she is ... although we're trying not to say that,' said Joe, still staring up at the photos, with what Kate assumed must be love in his eyes, although in truth, he just looked spaced out.

'What?' asked Pete, eyebrows excessively arched.

'"Beautiful", or, like, "pretty", or whatever – we're trying to, uh, y'know, praise her in non-gendered terms, for like, her mind, and her personality, and that kind of thing, for her self-worth, y'know?'

'Oh *wow*, that's so cool man,' said Pete, somehow raising his eyebrows even higher, seemingly *amazed* by this.

'Yeah, that's deadly,' repeated Tom blankly. He'd been texting someone on his phone as Joe spoke, but now placed it, with difficulty, back into his tightly stretched trouser pocket.

Maria returned, smiling simperingly. 'She's okay, her dodie had juss fallen out!'

'Aaaw,' said Joe, smiling back at her. Maria, pausing as she passed Joe's seat, put out her hand, into which, after the slightest pause, he placed his phone. Pressing the button along the side with her forefinger, she turned down the music until it was barely audible. Suddenly, they could all hear the dishwasher chugging in the kitchen, through the arch at the far end of the room.

'Hey babe, have you shown the guys some recent photos of Marta?' she asked, already typing in his password.

'Yeah love, I just did,' Joe lied.

'The one of her at the farm? Di' you show them that one, where she's looking ah deh piggy?'

'Yeah, I did.'

'And what about the one in deh little dress from my mother, the Frida Kahlo one?'

'Yeah!' Joe said, a faint hint of irritation in his voice.

'Oh, okay … great!' Maria said after a split-second pause, disappointed to have missed the opportunity to admire her daughter in company. Reluctantly, she handed him back his phone. As he returned it to his pocket, Kate saw him turn up the music with his thumb. Maria, who must have noticed too, said nothing, but continued hovering by his chair.

'She's gorgeous, Maria,' said Tom, placatingly.

'She's ah intelligent, kind, wonderful little girl, yes,' said Maria, forcing a smile. *Yes, we got that from the photos,* thought Kate. Again, there was a pause. Then Maria gathered herself: 'Anyone for a drink while I'm up?'

Maria pushed in the chairs around the dining table as she passed into the kitchen. When she was through the archway, Joe took out his phone and turned up the music again, grinning, and the two other guys grinned back.

Kate watched them. *Yes, an intelligent, kind, wonderful* … Maria's words ran in circles round her mind as she pictured (as she often did, to soothe herself) going up to each of these men, one by one, getting down on her knees, and gently easing out from their jeans their little, limp, wormy cocks, before taking them whole in her mouth and, in one swift motion, biting them clean off, before – *yes, you dreamt right boys* – swallowing. She gulped, almost feeling the warm, bloodied lumps of flesh disappearing down her throat. On Spotify, New Order started playing.

'Ah, *tune* ... The amazing thing about New Order, right, is that, like, actually, they weren't very talented instrumentalists ...'

'Yeah man! Exactly, that's why their sound is so crazy, they're like, self-taught, and so –'

'Iss so amazing, y'know, being a mama.' Maria was sitting down next to her, handing her a drink. Kate hadn't even noticed her come back into the room.

'Oh, uh, yeah, I'd imagine ... Must be amazing,' she said, startled.

'I still can really believe it, honessly ... like, I'm gonna be her mama for *life*, y'know? Gonna see her through all those important moments, like, when she meets someone or graduates or whatever, and I'm gonna have to do all her school lunches and like, hurt *knees* y'know? Iss crazy! Ha ha!' Maria was smiling, and yet there was something else there, a slight falter, a forcedness. Kate wondered for the first time if Maria found being a mother hard, if maybe she wished she could have someone to talk to about it. *Oh well*, she thought, sipping her drink and smiling back, *that someone ain't gonna be me.*

Here, in a swift, sharp motion outside of her control, Kate's mind flashed to her own mother's tearful face emerging from the toilet bowl, reaching out to Kate to help lift Mommy to bed, sobbing and spluttering, a little purplish trickle of sick running down her chin; flecks of it, too, she could see again now, just visible in the curving inverted sky of the toilet bowl, purple against white, the sight of which made Kate nauseous in turn, dizzy. Her mother's low guttural moans amplified as she lowered her head again, unassisted by Kate, who stood frozen in the doorway – yes, there she was, Kate could see herself now, with the distance of years; there was little kid Kate, small and skinny, with bed-knots in the back of her strawberry blonde hair, forever frozen in that doorway, the white downy fur of her arms raised from the chill of the air after bed, and from fear. Nose still button-shaped, more freckles than now, and those My Little Pony pyjamas.

Kate's mind skimmed yet again, in spite of her frantic internal urgings away from such recollections (but there was nothing to distract her; Maria was waffling on about supporting her daughter whatever she chose to be – gay, straight, bi, female, male, whatever made her *happy* – and Tom was avidly describing to the other guys the intricate pros and cons of various electric vehicles), across all the many times this scene, or some approximation of it, had occurred over the years, beginning when Kate was what – four, five? Standing there, scared, wondering was her mommy dying, should she call 999, until she got used to it, and it became regular enough for her not to be afraid. Slowly, she learned to harden her soul against her mother, to stay curled up in her bed and ignore those throaty, desperate cries clawing at her from the bathroom – clawing, clawing across the narrow landing, pulling and grasping under and around the edges of her firmly closed door.

Back then, to calm herself, Kate had begun thinking of this night-time apparition as a kind of monster, one who'd taken over the body and mind of her mother and who would usually, although not always, be gone the next morning, if she could only survive the night. Later, as she got older and more inured against such displays, Kate became, by an effort of sheer will, entirely indifferent. She trained herself in callousness, morphing terror into a kind of satisfied hate, and stopped even hearing her mother's sobbing. Eventually, her mother, after the first few desperate moans, learned to stop calling to her.

On some nights though, as Kate got older, if she knew she'd want a fiver the next day to go to McDonald's with some of the girls from school (all of whom seemed to work in digital marketing now, with boyfriends who were employed as 'creatives', or – like Pete, Joe and Tom – in tech), she would listen out for her mother's stumbling ascent of the stairs, her plaintive muttering and muffled coughs and, once she heard the heavy thud of flesh and bone collapsing onto the bathroom floor, Kate would get up from her warm bed and go to her. Resolutely ignoring her mother's blubberings (*thank you, baby* and *I'm so sorry* and *you're so good* and *you're the best thing that ever happened to me, my angel, the only good thing*, followed by many more half-burped *sorrys* and *oh Gods*), she would hold back her hair. And maybe, if she was hoping for a tenner rather than a fiver (for, say, a new lip gloss from Claire's Accessories plus McDonald's), Kate would even go so far as to rub her mother's back, and to coo gently, *it's all right, it's all right, you're all right Mom, just get it out, get it all out …*

Sitting there now on the black leather couch, the bells of St Patrick's Cathedral, just around the corner from the flat, faintly discernible under the Nils Frahm track playing, which in turn could just about be heard under the shrill hum of the group's chatter ('but seriously like, do you not think it's so immoral for these billionaires to be going up into space when the Earth is in crisis?' 'But space could be our only hope!'), Kate could hear and see and feel it now again – she was here, in the flat, but she was also back there, in her childhood home; she could hear, weaving its way through the layered noises of the present, the sound of her mother's hacking vomit, her gurgling, sniffling sobs, which seemed to rise through her body like oily black tides of sorrow, bubbling up from the very lowest pit within her. Kate could smell, above and through the metallic, slick, non-smell of the cocaine coating her nostrils, the sharp, tart taste of wine in her mouth, the faint tang of male sweat coming off the men, Maria's deodorant, and the vanilla candle she had lit, the scents of back then: acidic wine-sick, combined with the thick lemon bleach her mother always squirted into the toilet the morning after, and the damp of the shower curtain, which was patterned with jungle animals and still there from when she was a baby. There she was, perched on the couch beside Maria, and on the edge of the bath, behind the wide, curved back of her mother, who had one arm draped across the toilet seat, her thick legs splayed across the floor.

In the photos of Kate as a baby, and even as a toddler, her mother had been small and blonde, like Kate was now, but over the years she'd ballooned slowly, her large stomach growing hard and tumorous, her breasts long and flat. Her face, increasingly surrounded by jowls, had become shiny and waxen, almost translucent, exposing a network of thin blue veins across her cheeks, as though the skin there had not been designed to stretch so far. Her mother's small features, in that ever-widening face, looked more and more absurd as Kate got older, so tiny and lost were they in that mass of flesh – although Kate would only notice this when she left for significant periods of time before being forced to return, as happened with increasing regularity the older she got, when she began running away to boyfriends' houses as often as she could. There, safe for a while, she would play the part of the poor little broken girl to both the boys and their kind but cautious mothers, spilling out her sad stories of neglect and drunken chaos in return for home-cooked meals and a place to sleep in fresh, heavily scented sheets in the spare room or on the couch.

To Kate, these women had all now blurred into one vague memory, all with short brown hair and unflattering jeans from Dunnes Stores and leather Orla Kiely purses on the hall table. They were the wives and mothers who'd done it right, who were raising good boys, and wanted no uncomfortable realities to darken their sons' prospects; who wanted, above all, to shield them from the ugliness and the complex trouble a girl like Kate brought. It was always only a matter of time before Kate was exiled from their meticulously maintained homes, homes with kitchen gadgets lining the marble countertops and patio furniture that got covered in patio furniture-shaped tarpaulin to protect it over winter. They always had elegant front rooms that were only entered on special occasions and were invariably deathly cold and unwelcoming even when in use, unable to expel their air of stale emptiness after so many hours and days and months with the door firmly shut.

Actually, thinking back, Kate did remember one particular mother, an especially unhappy, especially cowering yet proud creature (unduly pleased with her semi-detached house, her average children, her good shoes, because otherwise what else would she have to keep afloat?). She was small like Kate, but hunched, although she must've only been in her early forties then. She used to spend her afternoons with her youngest child, a daughter born unexpectedly twelve years after her son, in the café of the local supermarket, always just the two of them, whispering secrets about nothing. One day, in the house alone on a Sunday, when the family had all gone out to mass, Kate wandered into this woman's room, with the intention of masturbating on her enormous, freshly made marital bed, and found, in the drawer of the father's bedside table, a carefully folded note:

> *Dear Alan,*
> *I know we have discussed it many times before, but please, I'm begging you, do not park the Jag in the driveway any more. As you know, it is leaving oil stains on the new paving, and I am going out of my mind.*
> *Love, Linda*

Kate's mother, for all her faults, was nothing like these women. For one thing, none of her feelings were hidden from view, even the ones that ought to have been. As her corpulence increased, the ever-starker contrast between her features and the face that housed them gave her a look of constant uncertainty or of disappointed surprise, as though she had just overheard someone say something mean about her – someone she thought was her friend. Often, this was her actual expression, since Kate's mother pretended to think everyone was her new best friend, purely so she could indulge in the anguished pleasure of having them all disappoint or betray her in the end. Her hair, after many bad dye jobs, had thinned, and was now stained a pinkish red, speckled with short, wiry, white strands at the roots that often stood on end from her parting. Her feet had always bothered her, but this had grown worse with the weight and the boozing, and was aggravated further by her work in the supermarket, until she'd been told by a doctor that if she didn't change her ways, she could face amputation of her lower left leg. Although she'd cried heartily at the news and sworn the usual resolutions, in effect it made little difference, although nowadays, she was obsessive about getting Kate to rub essential oils into her shins whenever she visited, which was rarely.

Besides, Kate's mother had gotten it into her head, probably from daytime TV, that apple cider vinegar was a miracle cure for all that ailed her, and so downed teaspoons of the stuff four or five times a day, even bringing her bottle and small plastic medical spoon to work with her. She did this, both in penance for the wine drunk the night before, and in preparation for the wine she would drink later on. She stuffed cotton balls between her curled and long-nailed toes in her black work shoes to stop them chafing against one another (she couldn't stay bent down long enough to cut them properly, and so there were little orange blood stains along the tops of all the socks she owned that weren't black or navy).

These days, other than for her work shifts, which had been reduced to three days a week, Kate's mother barely ever left her apartment, partly because it was easier to keep drinking that way, but also because she had grown so large that it was difficult for her to tackle the three flights of stairs down to the door, let alone the unknown amount of walking she might be faced with once she left the building. Kate knew she was self-conscious about her weight, could tell from the way she pulled at her cotton tops and floral blouses, and from how she glanced around nervously whenever they were out, terrified yet impelled to see the people who might be staring, agog, at the sheer mass of her body. Kate also knew that this was another reason she hated leaving her apartment, knowledge that ensured, due to some perverse aspect of Kate's personality, that on the rare occasion they did see one another now, Kate always insisted on first meeting her mother in a café or a park or a shopping centre. If she was feeling particularly cruel, she might say she needed some new underwear, and drag her mother along with her to the lingerie department in M&S, pulling out 26B-sized bras and size 8 thongs, and holding them against herself, just to watch her mother squirm in hot-cheeked discomfort.

Rarely, nowadays, would she deign to visit her mother in her home. Recently this had become even less likely, because (presumably due to the distinct lack of human affection in her life), her mother had adopted a cat, a strange and moody white Persian with inbred-looking glassy blue eyes, which had duly begun to shit in every corner and under the bed. With apparently no awareness of the Freudian implications, her mother had named this cat 'Kit', and spoke to it constantly, coyly remonstrating with it for being naughty or for bothering Kate, thus finding a means of exorcizing the underlying anxiety brought on by the real Kate's presence. When Kate complained about the stench, her mother said she was imagining it, and insisted the place was perfectly clean. Clearly, Kate concluded, her mother was too much of a drunk to notice, her sense of smell apparently dulled by years of bodily abuse. As far as Kate was concerned, the whole place fucking stank.

It was Kate's turn for the cocaine. Maria was poking her shoulder to take it.

'Oh! Thanks.'

Yes yes yes, come to mama ... Kate's face broke into a wide grin, and Maria furrowed her brow slightly, coolly alarmed. Wait, she had smiled, right? Or did she just bare her teeth?

'I know, I know, but the thing is, like, with every Google search you do, right, you're using enough energy to power a lightbulb for an *hour*.'

'I thought it was light a house for an hour?'

'I thought it was power a lightbulb for a minute?'

'But wait, I still don't get the Bitcoin thing, why's that worse for using up energy? Surely it's better than, like, printing a load of plastic credit cards and money and all that though, right?'

'Oh man, don't get me started on Bitcoin! Ethereum is the way to go man, seriously, I have this app, you need to get it –'

'I know! Honestly, in two hours I made –'

'No, wait, but that's not the *point*! The point is the planet can't withstand –'

The light in that bathroom was always so grim, Kate thought. She sat up and passed the now-emptied place mat along to Pete. Painful memories came fast and thick to her now like photos dropped from a height onto a table. Disengaged from her surroundings, she was instead coasting effortlessly and erratically from one old misery to the next, as she was wont to do whenever she drank or snorted this much, which these days was at least once a week.

She grimaced at the images, but also – she realized a fraction of a second later – the grimace came from the whoosh of cocaine hitting her brain, which she hadn't really noticed herself taking. With an effort, she heaved her focus back into the room. She looked over to see if Pete was laying out any more and, glancing up from doing so, he smiled at her in a way she thought was designed to look conspiratorial. *Huh, strange,* she thought. She was probably imagining it.

Tuning back into the conversation, she discerned that Tom was again dominating the talk: 'Oh my God, that's crazy, like, how have you not heard about them? They're incredible man, seriously, you need to check them out ... Right, so like, there's only gonna be a hundred or so pairs, and they're all black, but like, this beautiful, really dark black – no, seriously, look them up, it's some new dye, from the rainforest I think, but it's obviously being sourced, like, completely ethically, but it means they're, like, darker than any black before, and they have Mista Reeks's *actual blood* in the soles – yeah, I know, so cool, and the tick's in this like, gold thread, that I think has some gold from like, Aztec times weaved in – yeah, man, seriously! I'm not kidding! And they have a vertical line in red coming down through the centre of each tick, to be like, a cross, like – yeah exactly! Exactly, like Christ on the cross, 'cuz you know that Mista Reeks track, from, like, '96 I think, about being the Messiah come again and all that? Yeah, so like, it all ties in – they're like, metaphorical ... So fucking deadly ...'

'Doesn't he say in that song that he's gonna wreak havoc on the white people?'

'Yeah, but like, that's just a metaphor, he means, like, the *racist* white people.'

'Oh, right, cool ... they sound cool man.'

'They are, seriously, they're sick.'

They all sat in silence a moment, considering.

Kate looked up, and her gaze was caught by the motion of a fly that was edging its way in frenetic little steps here and there across the surface of the bulging paper lampshade that hovered over the centre of the room. She wondered if it was listening to everything they were saying and imagined that, if so, the fly must've thought they were fucking idiots.

'Kate?'

'Huh?' She blinked.

'I asked are you okay?'

It was Joe. He was in his seat across the way, a safe enough distance from which to address Kate without Maria suspecting any intimate intentions. Still, noticing, Maria paused in her flow of talk, now about the horrors of palm oil, and looked from one to the other, a little ripple of irritation passing across her brow. The room went momentarily quiet, other than the Fontaines D.C. remix now playing.

Life ain't always empty

Life ain't always empty …

'Huh, oh yeah! Ha, God yeah, I mean, well, it's just, I was thinking about, um, what Maria was saying, y'know, about …' Her mind jammed, shit, what had she been saying? 'About, uh, how terrible palm oil is.' She looked to Maria, scrambling to make sense of the jumble of barely heard words that had just been flowing across the outskirts of her ears. 'Like, you'd just never think it was in Jolson's Soap, that's so interesting, because, y'know, it's so old, Jolson's, like, so you'd think, wouldn't you, that the recipe would predate it?'

'Ah, but see dis is the ting!' Maria leapt on the affirmation of her own point, immediately forgetting her distrust of Kate, instead jubilantly delighted to have this encouragement. 'See, all these producers, righ', is like, they don't want you to know, righ', so they use different names on the labels, other than actually writin', like, *palm oil*, see? Because they're gonna use whatever is cheapest for them, y'know? Like, fuck the environment an' our children's futures, right? So like, take shampoo for example, any shampoo …'

Joe kept staring at Kate with a look of questioning concern, but Kate looked away, training her gaze instead on Maria, who would, she knew, keep talking now, whether she proffered any meaningful responses or not. Had she zoned out *that* thoroughly? Had it been noticeable? Now, Kate made the concerted effort to nod and occasionally said 'wow' or 'no way!' but she still wasn't quite listening. To be fair, they'd all stopped listening, and were now just waiting it out until Maria finally paused, and someone else could interject.

On Spotify, 'Lucifer' by Jay-Z started playing.

'Oh man, I *love* this song!' said Pete, accidentally on purpose interrupting Maria. His whole body seemed to swell, suddenly overwhelmed with joyful recognition. As the song got going, he began smiling and pointing at the air, almost levitating off his seat. 'I got them to play this at my brother's wedding, man, it was so fucking good, ha!'

'Is tha' deh one who got married in Sicily, oh my God, with deh crabs on the beach?' Maria asked, laughing. She seemed to have immediately forgotten that she'd been in the middle of listing various palm oil derivatives, happy to be able to reference a funny inside story with Pete, thus suggesting intimacy between them. Maria always got flirty when she was high.

'Nah nah, the one who married the preppy girl in Malibu,' Pete said, with a hint of a smirk.

'Oh, yeah, the other beach wedding, ha! You gonna have to marry someone on Sandymount Strand, Pete!'

'If an Irish girl will have me,' he grinned, his eyes flitting to Kate.

Jesus fucking Christ, thought Kate, tilting her head upwards to search for the fly again.

'Was tha' the girl with the billionaire daddy?' said Maria, diligently ignoring Pete's last comment.

'Ha ha, ah, he's not a billionaire,' Pete smiled, sucking his beer, his expression even more insufferably coy now, quietly delighted that she'd acknowledged the money.

'No, okay, only a multimillionaire then!' Maria shot back. Kate glanced at Joe; he was looking at Maria, a blank expression on his face. Pete shrugged, his smile intimating that he couldn't possibly say. There was nothing that excited people like Pete and Maria more, thought Kate, than the proximity of *big money.*

'Where did he get his millions from?' asked Kate, feigning innocent curiosity, even though she knew the answer – had heard the whole story already, the family background and the wedding itself, replete with all the extraordinarily decadent wedding costs and honeymoon costs and champagne costs and the surprise gift of a beachfront condo for the happy couple, unveiled only moments after they'd cut the cake.

There was a barely perceptible pause.

'Texas oil,' said Joe sharply. When she looked up at him, taken aback by his tone, he was gazing straight into her eyes before breaking away and looking back, safely, at Maria. Maria looked from Joe to Kate again, sensing something and not liking it (it was always the people who flirted inappropriately, Kate thought on some substratum of her mind, who assumed that everyone else was secretly flirting too). Although, admittedly, Kate could sense something strange passing between herself and Joe, but she didn't know what, exactly. Was he onto her? But then, if he knew she was mocking them, sitting here thinking mean thoughts, as she clearly was, did it really bother him? What did he think of it all, really, this money worship? This moralizing, as they sat here taking *cocaine,* sourced from who knew where, but definitely somewhere immoral, somewhere not exactly *eco-friendly*? Surely he must've found it just as gross as she did? Found his own hypocrisy just as disheartening as she found hers? But then, no, he wouldn't, of course. He'd be all in, and he'd be hurt that she wasn't all in too, hurt that she was sitting there, seeing it, silently scoffing. But these conversations were bullshit, even servile, she thought, angrily defensive, in their broken-spirited inability to diverge from the same old cycles of money, guilt, products, money, guilt, products. Okay, sure, they didn't have to be intellectuals, but where had the sense of humour gone? Her mind silently beseeched him, asking him, pleading. Where had the ability to talk about things other than prospective purchases and past purchases and TV shows and the end of the world gone? Do you remember when we used to make jokes, Joe? Or talk about books, or art, or even – God forfucking-bid – about thoughts, about the meaning of things, for Christ's sake? Whatever happened to meaning, Joe, do you remember that old stuffy fucking *notion*?

But then, even in her mind, this sounded stupid and pretentious. So maybe she was the problem, the one out of sync. Because, to be fair, the end of the world was coming soon, so she guessed it was probably only natural to talk about it constantly, right up until it actually happened.

She continued, as the strange moment passed, to glance over at Joe, hoping to catch his gaze again, to somehow apologize with her eyes – for what, she wasn't totally sure. But he didn't look back at her. Instead, he twisted the bottle in his hand and pretended to read the label for a moment, before busying himself with the proffered cocaine place mat, which was making the rounds again and had just landed in front of him. But he shouldn't get to make her feel bad, get to judge her – he's the one who used to rape her.

Oooh now, 'rape' is a bit strong, come on.

Okay, well, 'used to fuck her' then, without her consent.

Yeah, but she didn't say no either, remember, not really, not forcefully …

Eh, okay, well then, 'used to fuck her' … full stop?

Let's just say, whatever happened back then, he has no right to judge her now. But then, did he even judge her?

Well, his tone was sharp.

Maybe she imagined that? She is, I think it's fair to say, feeling a little weency bit paranoid …

Here, why don't you just shut the fuck up. How about that? Just shut up.

… Now that, *I'd say, was undeniably 'sharp'.*

Shut The Fuck Up!

'Jeez!'

'What?' Pete was looking at her.

'What?' Kate said, startled.

'You just said "jeez"?'

'Oh, uh …' Kate couldn't think of what to say. To explain that she'd been having a conversation in her head probably wouldn't sound great.

'Eh, I was just thinking about names for vegan cheese alternatives.'

'Oh! Cool! "Jeez", ha ha, that's a good one.' Pete smiled encouragingly, as one might smile at a terminally ill child who talked of their big plans for adulthood. Kate smiled back, before taking a deep gulp of her drink, again angling her body away from him.

This evening was going awry. She could feel it. It was all tipping slightly to the side. She needed to pull it back, pull *herself* back. Straighten up, be present, be *here*. More cocaine, she was sure, would help. Or, well, okay, maybe not *help*, but it would do something, propel time along, at the very least.

Here it comes now, coming now, c'mon baby, back around …

Maria handed her the mat, rubbing the last of her own line into her gums with the forefinger of her other hand.

There we are.

She put it on the arm of the couch, placed the rolled-up fiver in one nostril and covered the other with her finger. Leaning right over the place mat, she sniffed hard, moving the open end of the note carefully up along her line.

Ah. There now. Better.

Dabbing up any remnants with her finger, Kate passed the now empty place mat along again to Pete, the source. This time, he winked at her. He really, truly *winked*. She was sure of it.

Jesus, who was this guy, Jimmy Savile? He was like those old guys in bars when she was a teenager. Maybe things were different in America? She glanced at Joe, and although he appeared to be looking diligently at Maria, who was talking, she could tell by his thinned, disapproving lips that he had seen the interaction.

Ha!

It would never, ever happen. Pete was too broadly, textbook American; there was no darkness in his sense of humour, as in, nothing actually, deeply funny, and he worshipped money. Also, she would sooner die than get married on a beach. It would be like being proposed to in Paris, or Japan. Faced with getting married on a beach, she'd walk into the sea. It would simply never work out.

Besides, she didn't think she'd ever be able to bring herself to fuck him. She glanced at him, appraising; looking up from where he was neatly doling out yet more lines, he immediately caught her eye, winked again and smiled. *Fuck!* She shifted her body even further away from him, this time turning all the way around to Maria and resting her lower back against the armrest of the sofa.

Was there an Irish equivalent to a green card he was after? But then, surely he could meet some girl in work only *dying* to marry a big blonde yank and have his rich yankee-doodle babies? Maybe he thought Kate's quietness meant she was sweet and shy, a good little Irish wifey in the making, perfect to bring home to Maw and Paw.

But then, Kate was sweet and shy really, wasn't she? Deep down? Sort of? It was only tonight – or, well, only recently – that her thoughts were those of a total fucking bitch.

Ah, she told herself, *but all women are bitches when they're unhappy, just as all men are bastards when they're unhappy!*

God, she was so sick of being so desperately unhappy. So sick of being so desperately lonely. It was so hideously predictable, so clichéd, beyond anything else. Where had the happy people gone? The truly happy, rather than the Insta-happy, the performers, who all seemed to either live on a yoga mat or to have had their lips injected into semi-permanent Joker smiles. She'd love to find a happy person, someone contented with their lot, not forever striving. But they all appeared to have sunk into the past, last spotted in adverts for fizzy drinks in the '80s and early '90s. Where were they now, and why couldn't she be one of them? Kate felt her eyes welling in spite of herself. Maybe she should just go home, call it a night. Sipping the end of her wine, trying to make the ends of this glass last after her initial big gulp, she glanced around surreptitiously, hoping not to be noticed, to hide her face behind her hair. She saw, from the corner of her eye, Pete's hand proffering the mat to Tom, who grinned his thanks. *God,* Kate thought, *those lines look huge!* Spotify's algorithm decided on Al Green's 'Let's Stay Together' as their next track, and Kate felt her mood lift a little. She was very comfortable in her seat. After all, what was there to go home to? An empty room. A cold bed. Some desperately unsexy porn, to which she'd only just manage a weak, hissing splutter of an orgasm, at best. And besides, it was generally acknowledged that only stupid people ever really managed to be happy – so maybe she should be grateful for all this grey leaden misery. At least it proved that she was smart.

'Top up?' asked Maria, who, now that all the other white wine was gone, was hovering the bottle of Kate's shit, cheap Pinot Grigio over her glass.

Ah, sure what the hell, she'd stay a little longer.

Joe was talking about something. There he was, good old Joe, looking like a modern-day gimp, she thought, in his trendy jeans, with their yellow stitching and turned-up hems, his navy button-down, his white Reeboks. *God, he could be anyone.* Mostly, she forgot that this was the same Joe she'd known back in college, the one who'd fucked her when she was comatose. Back then, he'd dressed badly, in chequered shirts and boot-cut jeans from Penneys. He'd worn a permanent gold chain around his neck and those rubber charity bracelets on both wrists, revealing the country boy he was. Joe, who'd volunteered to go to Lourdes three years in a row at school, and who'd raised a lamb from infancy after its mother died giving birth, only to discover his father had sold it for meat along with all the others one day while he was out at football training.

Joe, who'd loved Jane Austen novels so much that he called himself Mr Darcy on MSN Messenger as a teenager. Joe, with whom she was once, briefly, before the fucking became this invisible emotional wall between them, actually close, and with whom she'd shared real intimacies, hopes and fears, at least a handful of times. She'd even told him about her mother, about the drinking; in turn, he'd told her how his older brother used to feel him up at night in the bed they shared when he was a little boy.

She generally forgot, now, that Joe knew anything about her, let alone the texture of her pussy. Just then, his eyes grazed hers, and she could see nothing in them. Nothing that implied any connection between them. And for the first time in what felt like years, that made her feel sad. If that Joe was completely gone from her – as she knew, in truth, he was – she really was totally alone here. She was near these bodies, breathing the same air, but apart, as though surrounded by a thin, cold film, invisible yet impenetrable.

As Pete grooved into the music in his seat, head down, even biting his lip a little (Daft Punk had started playing), Tom, suddenly remembering he'd been speaking at one point about something important, and feeling a surge of deep irritation at the constant interruptions, frowned, before resuming his thread from much earlier in the evening, talking even louder than before, 'So right, oat milk, yeah, okay, I know, but what I'm saying is –'

'No, but like, thaz serious, or even better is the pea milk, in the health food stores –' Maria interrupted him immediately, also effortlessly picking up where they'd left off hours ago, considering herself established now as Queen of the Evening, primary speaker, untouchable, her Spanish accent thickening with every passing minute. She had also decided, Kate noticed with a start, to pursue the conversational tactic of speaking quite *incredibly* loudly. Kate jumped in her seat, and looked over at her, amazed – was Maria actually shouting, or was she imagining it?

'– is difficult, but is not impossible,' she hollered, 'so yeah, Joe an' I, we get dis *pea* milk, 'cause like, is deh only one high in protein an –'

'Darling, the neighbours,' murmured Joe, leaning towards her.

Maria glared at him again and mouthed '*what*?' before turning her whole body to face away from him, aiming her attention across Kate to Pete and Tom, tilting her cleavage towards them, presumably to annoy Joe. Tom – who refused at this point in the evening to even pretend to acknowledge anything Maria said or did – continued talking, but much more quietly now, in deference to Joe. Pete, who'd finished grooving the moment the song ended (the Pixies had come on) stared at her tits, too fucked to realize he was even doing it or, it seemed, to comprehend what they actually were. His expression was one of stony seriousness, as though he were re-evaluating every one of his life choices, all as he gazed dolefully into those two rounded lumps of flesh heaving out of her t-shirt.

'Okay, yeah, yeah, I know, I know,' whispered Tom, speaking so low that they all had to strain to hear him, '… but what I'm sayin' is, that like, whatever about the milk thing, which is grand, and the meat thing, which is mostly fine, y'know like, so, yeah, whatever about them …' Tom paused here a moment, having lost his way again. He frowned again, looking around at each of their faces, his tongue readying itself for another word in his open mouth, eyebrows furrowed in the arrested development of his ability to think thoughts, before – ah, yes! His eyes lit up, satisfaction, there it was, his point, he found it: 'It's just that, I *can't* be gettin' on without *real cheese*, y'know?'

A pause, as Joe passed the half-emptied place mat to Maria, who smiled at him graciously – too graciously? Sarcastically so? – and, lifting it to just above her chest, immediately hunched over to snort the larger of the two remaining clean white lines. Everyone else breathed out heavily, before nodding reluctantly. They were embarrassed, frustrated even, at having to agree – even though they all knew what was coming, knew what Tom had been about to say, had known it before they'd even arrived there that night, felt like they'd known it before they'd even been *born*, since they'd had some version of this exact conversation every single time they'd met over the last two years.

'Ugh, I *know*,' said Joe dejectedly.

R.E.M. was playing now, a sad one. Its melancholic tones, combined with Tom's salient point, caused Pete to lower himself down into his seat, distraught, as if they'd finally reached the climactic crux of the matter, of all matters in the world, and there was no hope left. Delicious fucking bastard cheese.

And the night is yours alone ...

'Mmmm,' said Maria vaguely, reluctant to concede imperfect conduct on her own part, as she pinched some ticklish excess coke from her nostrils and passed the place mat along to Kate, who had been watching it go around again with beady-eyed intensity. At this stage of the night, Kate didn't give a shit about cheese, nor life, nor love, nor the impending end of the world – now, she only cared about the coke.

In fact, here was the undercurrent of thought, running below all the others, all through Kate's night, that had gotten louder and more prominent as the minutes ticked by: Pete was the one renewing the supply, and the place mat travelled clockwise, meaning she always got last choice of line. On some level, maybe four or five levels of her mind down, just below the level telling her to breathe, and the level telling her how to hold and raise a glass, to sip and swallow, and the level pretending to listen, and the level analysing it all, she was spending the entire evening in some obscure nebula of her brain judging which line looked the biggest, and then praying no one would take it before the place mat got back to her. Someone always did, of course – usually Tom or, if it survived him, Maria.

'I know what you mean,' the latter continued, unconsciously putting her hands down her top to reposition her breasts as she spoke, pressing them even further upwards in her padded t-shirt bra, as she began to do compulsively whenever she got this high.

'This is the thing, righ'? Because, like, they have no' made a good enough alternative, right? And dat is not our fault, y'know? Like, what are we suppose to do? In ah Spanish cooking, without *queso*, cheese, there is nothing, is no good, y'know? Is not right, an' like, thas juss how it is.'

'Right,' said Kate, who in turn was now staring, mesmerized, at Maria's large, raised breasts.

'Yeah,' said Joe, his despondency swiftly dissipating due to the medium-sized line he just snorted entering his bloodstream. In an instant he became animated, far more animated than usual, his pupils wildly dilated, and he spoke in tones ardently and needlessly defensive on Maria's behalf, the words spluttering out like vomit, with the meaning only coming later, if at all: 'I mean, me and Maria, we don't eat meat, or eggs –'

'Oh, thass true, we do dis scrambled tofu thing sometimes, where you –' Maria was speaking in a burst of excited animation (it was rushing through her now), sitting up and directing her words towards Kate, who looked up into her eyes, dazed into idiocy by her enthusiasm.

'Yeah, tofu eggs, we do!' Joe said, apparently enamoured with the memory, almost rising out of his seat, beaming at the room. 'It's so fucking delicious man, seriously like, you should try it –'

At this, feeling himself for no particular reason the primary addressee, Tom looked up from his phone's screen and nodded enthusiastically, 'I will man, I will, definitely –'

'You wan' some now?' asked Maria wide-eyed, sitting up quickly, readying herself to spring towards the kitchen.

'Uh ...'

'No, no, sorry, tha' was stupid, ha ha, sorry,' she said, giggling, lowering herself back into her seat again. A flicker of paranoia ran across her face and she shut her mouth tightly.

'And yeah, so ...' Joe continued, remembering mid-sentence the point he was trying to make, no longer smiling, but rather quite deadly serious, the cocaine spreading out silently through his bloodstream. 'Like, so, yeah ... so yeah, like, we drink pea milk and all that, of course, it's the least we could do, y'know? I mean, you guys saw those burnt animals ...' Here, a little nodded peace offering to Maria, who accepted it happily and nodded back. 'But like, the vegan cheese stuff – well, firstly, right,' Joe put his beer bottle carefully down on the floor beside his chair, before raising his spread fingers before himself, to better make his point, 'firstly, right, it's so terrible for you, *so* terrible, seriously like, it's all just *oil*, refined coconut oil, which is like, highly processed, so it's all just like, this awful saturated fat going into your body –'

'Like spackle for your bowels, honessly,' Maria said conspiratorially to Kate as Joe continued with his points, counting arbitrarily along his fingers. Kate had been watching the replenished place mat go around another time. She hadn't noticed herself taking her last line. Wait, had it skipped her? No, it couldn't have. She felt almost hypnotized from watching it, but edgy too, oddly enraged, as well as mellow, and frightened, and as though her whole body was melting into motion, yet stiffly unable to move a muscle. Not even pretending to listen any more, she murmured agreement with whatever Maria had said (spackle? What *was* spackle? Was that something to do with gluten?), but really, as no doubt they all knew (but fuck it, who cared?), she was too busy watching the coke. The rise and fall of every line, *like the cycle of life,* some part of her thought, which was quickly followed by another, more cogent part of her, embarrassed by the first part, who cringed, and quickly swatted the cliché away – *Jesus, no, not like the cycle of life, you dope* ... No, just itself, only itself, nothing else; the coke was the coke was the coke was the coke (*ha!*), which she'd now, in the midst of these thoughts, finished off yet again (*sniff!*), before yet again (*it's the ciiiircle of liiiife*) passing the empty place mat along to Pete, who would soon, all going smoothly, make more appear. *Ta-da!*

Good old Pete, the first part of Kate's mind thought now, briefly softening, *he's so nice, so generous, maybe I should marry him, actually, or at least suck his cock?*

Ha ha ha! the second part laughed. *Christ, you're a fucking riot,* it chuckled, slapping its internal knee.

This night was going *fabulously,* a third, apparently wildly flamboyant part of Kate's mind said, the sentence bubbling up out of nowhere, feather boa in tow. *Never have I ever had more fun than this!*

God, let that be a lie, said the first part.

Ignore her, she's fucking high, replied the second.

'Ha!' Kate exclaimed, before quickly covering her mouth with her hand. Luckily, nobody even noticed. They all seemed to be talking at once.

'So, like, what's actually the deal with installing heat pumps in gaffs? Like, are they gonna be worth the investment, d'ya think?'

'Oh man, don't talk to me, if I could afford a house in Dublin that ran on coal right now I'd fuckin' go for it, y'know?'

'Yesterday Marta was tryin' to say "I love you", I could see her lil lips goin', I know ih sounds crazy 'cause like, she's so young, but she is so advanced, she is so amazing, seriously, like, having a baby hass changed my life …'

'Wait man, I recognize this … Is this Little Simz? Have you listened to her latest? So good, isn't it? Honestly, I think the only truly interesting music being made now is by Black artists …'

The coke was at Tom now, sitting on the table in front of Tom, who was, as usual, taking his time getting to it, although he definitely fucking knew it was there, the cocky, muscly bastard. *Tom,* stupid idiot Tom, who could take all the time in the world if he wanted, and who got to choose his line first after Pete, *the lucky fucking swine,* Kate thought, burning up with sudden, plunging hatred, with his bulging arms and legs and his pimply little farmer's nose – *what an absolute prick.*

'I feel like what happened to Britney is just so indicative of our time, like, the whole thing, it just makes me so sad …'

'Yeah, Paris maybe, or New York, or Chicago, maybe, 'cause, like, wherever the jazz is, I'll just follow …'

Round again, a few times maybe, once, twice, a hundred times, she couldn't be sure, and back again at Tom now, of course – wait, was this the same time, or another? She needed a wee, but didn't dare go in case she missed her turn.

Casually, Tom leaned down over the coffee table from his perch on the footstool, rolled note in hand, and snorted up the biggest line, releasing a slight gasp afterwards, before pressing in each of his nostrils and sniffing hard to make sure he got it all. He then passed the place mat on to Joe, who didn't even notice it. Typical Joe, not really bothered with the substances, the drugs or the drink, but actually here for the *human company. Jesus,* thought Kate sarcastically, although deeper down, below her speaking mind, she envied him, and felt guilty for not being more like that: kinder, softer, more genuinely loving and open to others. *Oh well,* she thought, *we all have our foibles. Yeah,* said the other part of her mind, *and yours is that you're a mean cunt who hates everyone here.*

Yeah, exactly! said the first part.

Yeah, eh, and his is that he raped you?

Not that again!

Kate snorted into her drink. She looked around to see if anyone had seen her, and found Pete staring at her, grinning goofily, as though in on the joke.

'Joe,' Maria called gently, alerting him with a gesture to the cocaine on the table before him.

'Oh,' he said, putting down his fresh beer, 'don't mind if I do ...'

This made it, by Kate's calculations, halfway back to her again. But she'd already had a lot, maybe she should stop? How much was too much? Then, before she could decide one way or the other, it was before her on the table, the last surviving line, and she decided that she'd only know she'd had enough, or too much, if she kept going – so she'd simply have to keep going until she knew.

Ha ha ha, you eejit! That's how people die!

Ah well sure, what a way to go! Like Hendrix!

She inhaled quickly through her nose, her sinuses humming warm and sharp, and tried to subtly rub her nostrils, before lowering her fingers to her side to see, out of the corner of her eye, if there were any traces of blood. No, they were clear. God, of course there wasn't any blood. Fucking dope.

Calm down, Kate, she thought.

Wait, when did I stop being calm? She felt a shiver of apprehension run up her spine, a faint panic at realizing herself dangerously on edge. Inside her head, she pictured her mind pulling at its little imaginary collar.

Sure when are you ever calm, you mad bitch? she pictured the other part replying, casual and smooth, kicking back and smoking a cigar in the bath.

Don't worry about it, you're safe, you're grand, you're amongst friends, you're safe, you're grand ... intoned a warm, Santa-like part.

But why is it sometimes 'amongst' and sometimes 'among'? Have I been using them the wrong way all this time?

Never mind that now, you fool, just chill the fuck out – breathe, would yuh? reassured an oddly comforting part of her mind, this one in a tracksuit, decidedly Northside Dublin, but of the trustworthy variety.

Okay, yes, right, that's better ...

Kate breathed in and out slowly through her mouth. She felt jittery, giddy and jittery, the beginnings of the wonderful, no, horrible, no, *wonderful* immediate post-snort feeling, *ah,* just starting to seep down into the moments-later feeling of lavish decadence – the *Life Is A Gift From God* feeling; that transient, illusory sensation of complete contentment, held so briefly before inevitably and devastatingly slipping out of grasp, leaving only chasmous darkness peopled with all of her own particular mummified regrets, rising, arms outstretched, from the blackness.

'Here, did yiz see that movie, the one about a pig, or something, Joaquin Phoenix was involved with?'

'Oh yeah! No, I haven't seen it but I'd love to –'

'Hiccup! Oh, woops, ha ha, excuse me, acid reflex, I –'

'Oh, yeah, it's on Netflix, or Prime, is it?'

'Yeah, apparently the guy, the director, got him involved, because of that Oscar speech –'

'The vegan one?'

'Yeah!'

'I haven't heard of this, what is this?'

'Hiccup! Oh my God, sorry, they'll be gone in a minute, it's just when I –'

'It was out last year, it's like, a movie about a pig and how it grows up and is this, y'know like, proper sentient being and –'

'*Gunda*.'

'Oh God! I would cry watching that – I love piggies! Don' I Joe? Whass it called?'

'Yeah, she does, she loves piggies –'

'Yeah I just watched it last night, heavy goin' like –'

'Hiccup!'

'*Gunda*.'

'Yeah, absolutely.'

'Hiccup!'

'– need tissues! Ha!'

'*Gunda*.'

'What?'

'Hiccup!'

And what would her mother be doing now? Sitting home alone, Kit the cat curled up on her lap, or more likely shitting in a corner, while her mother, oblivious, watched TV, working her way through her second or maybe third bottle of the night. Kate could see the light from the images playing across her face, the blues and reds and greens, dancing, laughter jangling from the screen, the studio set's lightness and joy pulsing weakly into the darkness of the still, empty room. And her mother's enormous form, still too, except for the regular raising of the glass, the heavy breathing, and the slight shifting of her left leg, which would be hurting her now, as it always did. There she'd be, getting drunker by the second, more maudlin, but quiet, sitting quiet and hopeful that her phone, there on the arm of her chair, might light up with a text from her daughter.

Waiting in vain, Kate thought as her heart – she was sure – audibly cracked.

Now, as she sat longing for yet more coke, if only to stem this onslaught of horror, she watched, with all of her fierce will trained in its direction, as it made its way too slowly around the room. Yet even as she forced herself to focus on the simple, manageable fact of its trajectory, there were hints of that blackened mire, the sludgy, ragged presences of self-loathing and nausea and despair that she knew were coming for her, on their way even now – on their way from the moment she first lowered her head to the tomato sauce-stained place mat. Whether she stopped for them or not, they'd definitely fucking stop for her: those feelings, recollections, analyses of things said and gestures made. She shivered from the faint breeze of them across her spine, comprehension beginning to churn in her stomach. The sense of futility, her own, and that of the world's, the brief time she had, and all the ways in which she was wasting it, wasting it irrevocably. A writer! Ha! She was good for nothing ... And yes, there they were, she could see the gleaming edges of them now; all the fears of things said, from years ago some of them, others more recent, and how she'd been perceived, and how she must've been mocked, hated, dismissed – and now, what was she left with, in defence of all this? Her snide little comments, her disdain; *God*, it must be so apparent, dripping off her, *hateful little bitch*, with a mother she never got her fill of punishing, and no friends of her own, and no one to love her; the only place she was ever invited was here, where she came week after week, asked to come out of nothing but pure pity.

These thoughts, she knew, would overpower her tonight in bed, wrestle her down and dig their ugly, dead elbows into her chest, making her writhe and sweat and grind her teeth to flints. And they would only thicken and deepen when morning came, their effects less frantic but more depressingly denuding, stripping her soul down, however much daytime TV she watched or supermarket-branded muesli she ate. And they would not fully dissipate until Wednesday or Thursday, halfway through yet another week in the café, as she wiped down crumbs and ketchup from a table and listened (finding herself mouthing along to the words against her will) to terrible pop music on the radio, forever tuned to SPIN 1038 by strict orders of the boss. Only then, probably around 2 p.m. on Thursday, would the feelings of shame and horror begin to transmogrify into a sense of giddy relief at the prospect of another forthcoming weekend – a weekend when, who knows, maybe everything would change.

For now, though, maybe more cocaine really would help. Stave off the inevitable, at least. Right? What was that thing *utter fucking gobshites* liked to say – you only live once?

What time was it, anyway? She glanced at Maria's phone, which Maria was holding up during a lull in the conversation, scrolling through the Instagram of her cousin, the model back in Spain, the one she had all the hang-ups about. Maria was pretty, but certainly not stunning, with a strong Roman nose and big hips. Also, like Kate, she was extremely short – it was the only way in which they were physically similar. Kate was small and blonde and skinny, but she had a moon-face, with big blue eyes and small, baby doll lips. If she could have chosen, she would have been tall and dark and impressive, with black eyes and blacker hair and sharp cheekbones above deep hollows. In her dream world, she would have liked to be devastatingly beautiful – frighteningly so. She would have liked to be the kind of woman who made men feel lost for words and would have taken pleasure in being kind to them, putting them at their ease, by offering a gentle, soothing benevolence, in all the ways they never chose to offer her.

Some, of course, she would have been horrifically cruel to, but only the really simpering, sycophantic ones who deserved it. Like Tom, and Pete, and Joe. And even they'd only have loved her more for it, seeing as, being so dazzlingly beautiful, cruelty towards them would've been considered only natural.

Maria was slightly obsessed with this model cousin, and liked to talk at length about how her mother always compared them unfavourably, even now calling Maria 'my little tomato' and her cousin, 'my little cucumber'. The point of this admission, which Maria offered loudly and repeatedly with wide eyes, was that her interlocutor was supposed to rush to reassure her, tell her that she was just as beautiful as her cousin. If anything, they were supposed to say, she was more *real*, less 'magazine pretty' or whatever. This was a lie, and Kate, in particular, hated the misuse of the word 'real' amongst women, which she recognized as a patronizing and syrupy synonym for 'chubby', and which, concordantly, suggested that naturally skinny women like Kate (who couldn't do anything about her bony, childlike body) were 'unreal', somehow. But regardless, this was a lie Maria enjoyed hearing, repeatedly, from whomever she might meet. Kate stared at the screen, which was filled with bright beach and yacht and lakeside scenes, which in turn were foregrounded by white smiles, tanned skin, bikinis – more and more pictures of the same svelte, hairless body clad in various bikinis and, occasionally, skin-tight minidresses. More than anything, Kate's feeling was one of mild disgust, or maybe just simple despair, at the neediness of it all. It felt not unlike looking straight at the bloodied gashes on a girl's wrist. The poses were so contrived, so determined, and who were they for, really? For Kate? For Maria? Or for themselves, as young women liked to so deludedly claim? It was terribly sad, feminism gone wrong, Kate thought. But Christ, there was no denying it, she was absolutely fucking stunning, this girl. She found herself, even while denouncing the whole thing in her mind, unable to stop staring.

'Is that your cousin, Natalie?' she asked, pretending not to know, and feeling, as her mouth formed the question, a sore, red-raw patch where her teeth had ground against her inner cheek. Maria turned to her rapidly, her whole body jerking round, making Kate start.

'Yes – have I no' told you? She has just landed a campaign for Fendi. Is terrible, look, she muss no' be eating, she is too fahking skinny, righ'? I mean, look ah her *bones* here.' Maria zoomed in on an exposed hip bone, which, Kate conceded with a solemn nod, jutted sharply from her smooth, tanned skin. Looking at it, in spite of herself, Kate felt a vague stirring of warmth between her legs. Such a gorgeous body, she wanted to reach out and stroke its sun-warmed skin, taste its sweet saltiness, nestle her fingers in all its soft, wet goodness and health …

'Yeah, exacly, righ'?' said Maria, sighing, blotting out the screen of her phone with a press of her thumb and putting it back on the coffee table face down. Taking a large sip of her wine, she continued: 'It is juss so sad, der is nobody there to help her, I guess … I am so lucky I have Joe, she has no boyfriend, y'know, to mind her? And I am so happy that we are raisin' Marta not to care so much abou' her looks, an' to be a feminist … because it can be so destructive, y'know, like, is a curse for women, all this.' She gestured at the back of the phone, her hand denoting all the everything and nothing of the world contained therein.

'Yes,' said Kate blankly. She and Maria watched Joe come back from the bathroom, his fly unzipped. He was already losing his hair, Kate noticed, seeing for the first time the beginning of recession along his forehead as he bent forward to sit. This made her both happy and sad at once, before she swallowed both responses down with a deep gulp from her glass. If he was getting older, then so was she.

Pete and Tom were discussing Chelsea's chances in the Premier League. Pete had made a point of getting into soccer as soon as he found out he was being transferred to Ireland from San Francisco three years before, and had chosen Chelsea as his team because that was his sister's name. He was now a firm convert, and had even gone to London a few times to attend matches, buying a scarf and screaming and getting hammered along with everyone else. He also watched rugby now, and supported Ireland fiercely in the Six Nations and the World Cup. Although he didn't have to give up any of his old loyalties, since every guy in the office was obsessed with American football too, of course. The whole office had a huge late-night party to watch the Super Bowl, held in the building, with free American-style finger foods, including McDonald's. This buffet had been dubbed 'Trump's Treats' in the office WhatsApp group years ago, because back when Trump had tweeted a photo of the McDonald's he'd ordered in for a college football team visiting the White House, it had looked uncannily similar to the spread they put on at the office. Someone had made a meme pointing this out, putting the boss's head on Trump's and captioning it, 'A taste of America, anyone???' which was then reshared every year, and built upon, with more and more obscure in-joke captions, all of which generally got a good laugh amongst the group's participants.

Everyone in the office was, officially, in the WhatsApp group – it was an office requirement, designed to encourage bonding – but it was a core seven or eight people who actually kept it going. The rest were mostly silent observers. Only two, as far as they all knew, had gone as far as muting it. These were the guy from Oslo who worked in design and made techno music in his spare time at home, and that woman from Tipperary who worked in accounts, who was widely considered to be a total dry shite, and only ever got remotely animated when asked about her two pet spaniels, Jack-Jack and John-Joe. Some of the guys watched baseball, and some cricket, most notably the three Indian members of the team, who – although they hadn't dared mute the WhatsApp group, occasionally offering thumbs up or laughing crying emojis where required – tended to keep to themselves, eating together at lunch and socializing with one another, along with their wives and kids, on weekends. The Canadians watched ice hockey, but nobody else either watched or was willing to talk about it, since no one felt the need to impress the Canadians. Only a few of the women in the office watched sports; because of the dictates of the modern office environment, specifically that of 'equality', they were tolerated and, at least on the surface, encouraged by the men. The ones who got really into it, attending matches and participating in the office Fantasy League, were secretly considered suck-ups by the other women, who believed themselves honest enough to admit that all sports were, essentially, boring. These women, who listened to the same discursive podcasts on topics such as periods, depression and mothering, and who'd passed around a well-worn copy of the latest Dolly Alderton book, loved nothing more than riling up the guys by rolling their eyes whenever one or another team or league or cup came up in conversation. They were under the false impression that this came across as cute and sassy, like the cheeky, spunky women depicted in the romantic comedy movies they'd grown up watching in the nineties and early noughties (movies that were, unbeknownst to them, mostly written by single women).

'Another drink, anyone?' asked Joe, sitting forward in his seat and rubbing his hands together like people do in films.

'Ah, I dunno, I think they're in with a fair chance this year …'

'Babe, your fly,' smiled Maria, stage whispering to ensure everyone would notice. She turned back to roll her eyes at Kate, as though to say 'men, aye?' but Kate pretended not to understand. Her face, still unconsciously turned towards Joe's hairline, was resolutely vacant.

'Oh! Ha!' He leaned back to zip himself up, grinning at both of the women on the couch. 'Thanks love.'

'I'll have a drink please, Joe,' Kate said. She finished off the wine remaining in her glass, tipping it back, before sitting forward and presenting it. She thought she detected a little glance between Joe and Maria as he leaned over to take it from her, but decided it must be the cocaine making her see things. It had that tendency, she soothed herself, dismissing the nervous sensation tingling across her skin as she sat back into the warm safety of her nook.

'Like, yeah, okay, they say "biodegradable" on the label, but does that mean weeks, months, years? I mean technically, everything is biodegradable, if we're talking about, like, thousands upon, like, *gazillions* of years. I just wanna be like, c'mon Tesco, we need a little more transparency here, right?'

'You should call them out on X, man, make them accountable for their actions.'

'I might y'know, I really might, 'cause it's so important like, and I mean, no one seems to be asking these questions.'

'Yeah man, you should do it, seriously.'

'They'd never answer me though.'

'They would, man! They would, they have to on X, because like, the world is watching on there, y'know?'

'Mmmm, maybe … I dunno. It'd probably be pointless, they'd just give some bullshit answer.'

'Wait, is everything biodegradable eventually? Is that true?'

'Yeah, like, everything wears away in the end – right? Like, even fucking Newgrange or, like, the Colosseum will just collapse or, like, drift away some day.'

'Not plastic though.'

'Yeah, even plastic … but, like, the world will probably end first.'

'Is in our food, you know, in our ah-stomachs, and now they're sayin' liddle babies are drinking ih with their bottles, like, if they're no' breassfed –'

'Dude, you should message Tesco right now, see what they have to say for themselves.'

'All the supermarkets, man! Blitz the fuckers! Start a conversation!'

'Isn't that so terrible, though? Like, I am so glad that I breassfed Marta, 'cause like, that's so sad for those poor childre –'

'Yeah and like, all that nuclear waste they've buried all over the place, it'll take, like, forever, but even that will just, like, *long* after we're all gone, melt away.'

'Yeah, and now they're putting it in space, like, as if fucking up this planet wasn't enough, right?'

'Yeah, but sure we'll all be long dead by the time –'

'Oh yeah, totally, everyone'll be dead.'

'Even we're biodegradable!'

'Definitely.'

'Right.'

'Hey you guys, shudup, shudup a second – is that the baby?'

Pause.

Silence.

'Phew! God, I am way too high to go to her right now, ha ha!'

Kate was getting a bit angsty again. She wished they'd hurry up, stop pausing to listen and to speak, and just pass the fucking coke.

Oh yeah, that'd be fun Kate, no talking at all, just sitting here in silence, passing around cocaine until one of you dies.

Well, actually, that doesn't sound so …

'What are you smiling about?' she heard Joe ask through the smog of her mind, but she pretended not to have heard him. 'Let's Dance' by Bowie started playing on Spotify, and she felt immediately, radiantly becalmed, like the sound of his voice was sending soft, warm caramel all through her veins. She felt herself gyrating, ever so slightly, there on the couch. *Put on your red shoes …* Next thing, the coke was before her, and she dove down into it, snuffling hungrily for it like a little truffle pig with its nose in the dirt.

She felt, at the precise moment it entered her, clean, clear, like an electric car in one of those adverts, gliding smoothly around scenic cliff edges: spotless, gleaming, perfect.

Without warning, she saw her mother's face, smiling, holding Kate at arm's length before pulling her in close, enveloping her in her big arms in a warm, loving embrace, telling her how proud she was of her, her little Katie-doodie, all grown up, so proud, although for what, Kate could not remember.

Katie-doodie – God, she'd forgotten her mother called her that. Where had that come from? Something she'd said as a toddler, a picture she'd drawn for her mother, that she'd tried and failed to call a 'Katie doodle'.

She had completely forgotten that …

Her heart lurched painfully in her chest. How fast was it beating? Jesus, was she okay?

Sensing panic, she forced herself to surface out of the murky waters of memory to the bright, rigid shape of here and now, to slow her heartbeat. She focused on the blood whooshing through her veins and tried to slow it, breathing steadily through her nose, in and out, in and out. She closed her eyes and forced herself to picture her veins as rivers, blue rivers running all across a continent, bringing life to all the corners of her own personal land mass, travelling quietly and diligently all over her still, safe, living body – safe, she was safe, still living, here, now, safe. *Breathe*.

Honestly, though, was there anything in the world better than listening to Bowie? She wished they were all dancing, but equally, she never wanted to move from her seat, never ever again. If she'd been pulled up from where she was sitting at that moment, she'd have kicked and screamed and forced herself to die, right there, flailing herself to death on the ground like a child having a tantrum in a supermarket. But she wished she was dancing too. *Yes, dancing, yes, let's* – she beamed, the thought blossoming outwards as she felt herself overcome with a sudden and glorious joy.

'Just smiling!' she announced to Joe, sending waves of her happiness across to him – but he must have asked his question a long time ago, because he barely registered her response, sending a quick slight frown of confusion her way, before turning back to his conversation. He was talking animatedly yet quietly with Tom, something about a boss of theirs in work who was having an affair with someone on Joe's team. Pete, too, was making a show of listening, but Kate could tell at a single glance that he was too high to really comprehend the conversation, let alone contribute. He was gurning heavily, his eyes dreamy, and his head kept flopping slightly to the side before he snapped it back up into place again and resumed playing his role of 'listening intently'. Maria, she saw now, was not there, and had maybe gone to the bathroom, or to fix more drinks, or to put on more make-up, which she tended to do late into the night, anxiously wanting to up the ante in attracting male attention, all attempts at subtlety or propriety or shame long burnt off.

Kate didn't mind whether Joe heard her or not, she was easy – for now, she was sated. She bopped away, not really listening to anything but the music, not bothered by anything, sitting there in the soft folds of the couch. She caught Pete's eye. He was now busy making more lines, still gurning. He smiled back at her smiling face, bopped too, and she turned then – happily, dreamily – to Maria, who had reappeared at some point, lips thickly red and gleaming. Kate smiled to her and she smiled back, her legs tucked under her in the opposite corner, mirroring Kate in hers. God, wasn't everything wonderful? Wasn't life beautiful sometimes? And in that moment Kate felt – admiring her juicy red lips, her soft smile, soft skin – a surge of love for Maria, this woman who, whatever else, invited Kate back to her home, this apartment, time and time again, in spite of Kate's excessive consumption, her freeloading, and her general bad attitude. On a few occasions, Kate had drunk or taken so much here, or on a night out, that Maria and Joe had been obliged to carry her home and lay her down on this very couch to sleep it off. (Maria, whether due to intuition or possessiveness, or both, never allowed Joe to take Kate back to her own place, insisting she might fall on the stairs, or choke on her own vomit.) And Kate always woke up with a blanket thrown across her and a glass of water left out. And Maria never mentioned it, never complained, at least not to Kate. That was good breeding, that was very kind, very polite, Kate thought now, admiringly, bursting with gratitude and penitence. She wanted, in that moment, staring at Maria, who was looking over at Joe now, her smile turned instead towards him, to lean over and kiss her hard on the mouth. In a wave of arousal, she suddenly wanted to kiss each and every one of them, even Joe, even stupid gormless Pete, even silly muscly consumerist Tom. She wanted to undress each one of them, to have them undress her, to all undress each other, quickly, frantically, and then to fuck each other, in and out, all wet and warm and beautiful, and for them to fuck away the rest of the night like that, bodies melting into one entity, sweaty and gushing and beautiful. She wanted them all to take pleasure in one another, fast at first and then slowly, lovingly, and for them all – at dawn, maybe? – to orgasm all together, one great howl of perfection, the only perfection living humans were allowed in their bodies, all experienced in a perfect unison, the sun pouring in, turning each of them a golden-hued orange in their one big, fleshy mass of pleasure.

Why don't we? she wondered, genuinely at a loss, pushing the thought out on brainwaves of psychic interconnectivity. She tried to emphasize the obvious truth of this silent query by looking earnestly around her at all of those gorgeous, ravishingly perfect faces and bodies. But alas, she met the gaze of nobody. 'Let's Dance' ended, replaced by Spotify's algorithm with 'Smack My Bitch Up'. With it, the rush of desire dissipated.

Besides, there were all the usual hurdles, she thought, grimacing unconsciously as the aggression of the song penetrated her ears. Manners, awkwardness, inhibitions, possessiveness, fear of regret ... that's why it would never happen. And anyway, these people, these guys, she thought, glancing at Joe, Tom and Pete, who were watching a video on Tom's phone now and guffawing stupidly – they would never participate in the way she envisioned it; they would need to pursue power, to take control and make themselves known as the ones with the cocks, the strong ones, the *big men.* They'd refuse to touch each other, and make their focus the domination of the girls. And Maria would wiggle her ass and squeeze her tits together and moan, she'd pretend to choke deepthroating each of them in turn and would generally act like she was in her own, personal porno film. And this was not at all what Kate had imagined, in her brief vision of their perfect, equal union. That was the thing about sex, she thought, her mood darkening – people ended up performing, out of discomfort or fear or whatever, and that ruined it. Yeah, sure, you could still come, you could almost always come, with enough filth and fantasizing, but it wasn't this beautiful thing, this present absolute thing, the way she dreamed it. It wasn't the soft envelopment of bodies by other bodies; the wet, warm melting into one another, of tongues, thighs, lips, assholes, all of it, flooding into one easy togetherness. And maybe that, the thing she pictured, maybe that was 'lovemaking'. And if it was, she realized, sitting there, then she wanted to experience it. To experience it in its rich totality. She wanted to find someone, some perfect, imperfect anyone, man or woman, who would not just fuck her hard and fast or pointedly slowly, who would not count out the minutes they had to lick her out before they could stick their dick in her, nor lick her out excessively just to convey to her how evolved they were. Someone who wouldn't whisper trite banalities about her exceptional beauty in her ear as they entered her, nor tell her how much they're *loving it, baby, yeah, bitch, yeah baby, just like that.* Rather, someone who, wordless, would combine their body with hers in a sort of golden, circling unity, to create a feeling of wholeness she'd always felt was lacking, a oneness she craved intensely, to fill what was negative in her with what was positive in them, and vice versa.

And that person must be out there, right now, she thought, amazed. *I don't know them, have never met them – but they're there, walking, talking, eating, with their own personal history, their own quirks and scars and ways of seeing.*

And what if I never find them?

Her mother had never found her person. And you couldn't say she hadn't tried. All those awful men, always coming and going, marking off set periods of Kate's childhood: the quiet one with the moustache who drank Newcastle Brown Ale; the one obsessed with all things Steely Dan; the one with the blue Morris Minor who took them to classic car shows on Sundays; the one who shouted 'I'm fucking coming!' every time he came in the next room, as though otherwise Kate and her mother might accidentally miss it.

And Christ, how sad it was, Kate thought, suddenly overpowered by a wave of despair that crashed down around her before lifting her away in its cold brutal force, that these people here most likely won't ever experience this dream of idealized consummation, this one perfect thing our bodies can do, can know. All these good healthy bodies and souls sitting here around her, sitting pent up in their clothes, in rules and propriety and social codes, *wasted*, with so little time, really, to live, to touch and feel and experience such pleasure, before we all age: sag, wrinkle, stiffen, sink into decrepitude, and finally … Or maybe they all did, in their free time, in their own, private sex lives, manage something like what she was imagining? Maybe she was the only one left out? Kate looked around and caught Tom yet again unconsciously flexing, while Pete tried to surreptitiously pick his nose. Seeing Kate see him, he quickly pretended to have only been rubbing it.

No, she thought. Definitely not. All these good bodies, and no way to connect them. Jesus, it was a tragedy.

And she had the thought again, the one that plagued her, whenever she lost the strength to block it out: that this, now, all the nows always passing, every second, were a missed opportunity. This again was one of all the many missed opportunities that seemed to increasingly make up her days, all a long, sad nothing of doing the right thing or, more accurately, the normal, expected thing: walking from A to B to catch this train and not be late for that appointment, watching the numbers on a screen representing abstract concepts of money in her bank account, money that wasn't really there, going up and down with each month's earnings and spendings, and sleeping at night because that's when everyone else did it, always too tired in the evenings to write, or to do much at all but distract herself from the misery of the day with some telly, some light phone scrolling, along with a drink or three or five.

No, it wasn't misery, that would at least be something; it was the sheer nothingness, then, the void, where living, breathing, vibrantly experienced days ought to have been. And again, and again, the same, week in, year out, while all around her she knew, at every moment, were these veiled, indiscernible missed opportunities for touch, for wild excitement, for strength, for overwhelming sensation, for power, for love. Being alive is being touched, she thought then, almost crying at the thought. And when do I get touched? Her mind thrust her back into her mother's embrace, her Katie-doodie, and she thought for a moment that she might actually be sick, so overcome was she by longing.

She looked over beseechingly to Tom and Joe, who had paused their conversation a moment, for Tom to snort his fresh line. *God, how many times had it gone around now, twelve, forty?* Catching Joe's gaze, he grinned broadly at her, his eyes dazed from drugs and booze, his raised eyebrows implying 'why so serious?', even tilting his head slightly, which brought her back to their classes together, sharing a silent joke across the room. And then, from nowhere, Kate could feel his body climbing on top of her in the darkness, his heavy breathing, the press of his cock, first through the material of their clothes, then its taut hard skin pushing against her bare stomach, with his wet, hot slobber on her face and neck, her breasts, the force of his hands pulling at her skirt or the fly of her jeans, pushing open her legs, then pressing himself into her, the sharp stinging rub of dry hard flesh against dry inner flesh, only a lick of his saliva to moisten the blow. She shuddered involuntarily and looked away, not answering his smile.

No, not these people, these would never be her people. Never could she share such a thought, a revelation, with people like him.

'Less go out dancing!' yelped Maria, as though awoken from a sleep, thrusting her body up to the edge of her seat towards the boys, arms outflung. Drunk and high, Joe was continuing to stare openly at Kate as she made a point of looking anywhere else, hoping he would realize and desist.

Where has that fly got to?

'Where could we go?' asked Pete, still bopping and gurning. 'It's like ...' He raised his chunky silver Rolex and squinted a moment at its face. 'Wait, it's eleven-thirty already? No way! It couldn't be, is it? Wow. I thought it was only like, eight maybe.'

'Anywhere! Ha!' Maria was jumping up and down now on the edge of the couch, her hands clenched together.

Shaking himself into awareness and forcing his eyes towards Maria, Joe asked, 'What about Marta?' There was a hint of irritation in his voice.

'I already assed Josie, she said she'll watch her,' answered Maria, not looking at him.

'What? When did you do that?'

'Who's Josie?' Tom asked, looking from Maria to Joe, intrigued.

'She's our neighbour,' said Maria, 'she absolutely *loves* Marta.'

'I'm not a hundred per cent sure about her,' said Joe, quietly.

'What are you talkin' about Joe? She's amazing!'

'She's a pothead, Maria.'

'Yeah, and like, weird that she's up for minding a baby at eleven-thirty at night, amirite?' sniggered Tom.

'Pot and kettle are bode black, *Joe.* And I've been payin' her to be on standby since ten,' said Maria curtly, not looking at either Joe or Tom.

'What?' said Joe, taken aback.

'Wait, do you mean, the pot calling the kettle black?' asked Pete, genuinely confused.

'In case we wen' out,' she shrugged, answering Joe and ignoring Pete, 'wha' does it matter? It means she's there watchin' TV if we need her, she can just come roun' in her pychamas, no big deal.'

'But what if we didn't go out?' Joe laughed incredulously.

'What? I pay her. Is no' a big deal – truss me, is happened before.' Maria was getting irritated now, defensive. She flicked her hair threateningly. There was a pause.

'So, uh … where could we go?' Pete asked again.

'We could go to lohs of places, Ukiyo Bar, or Dicey's?' answered Maria, who was already beginning to scrabble around for her shoes.

'Friends of mine are having a rave up on the Northside actually, should be a late one, all-nighter maybe,' said Tom, tentatively.

Kate rolled her eyes. Everyone in Dublin pretended they were friends with anyone who made them look cooler than they were; this categorization could change on any given night. Really, everyone just knew each other to see, and stalked one another on social media to ensure they all knew what secret, low-key, 'exclusive' events were happening, *along with everybody else in the city.*

'Oh! That's so perfect, a rave! Amazing, I'ma textin' Josie now.' She was already reaching for her phone.

'Cool, so … I'll arrange a taxi then?' Tom looked to Joe.

'Oh yeah,' said Pete, nodding enthusiastically, 'I think I heard about that, Dave and those lads are putting it on, right?'

'Yeah, that's it,' said Tom, still looking at Joe for the official go-ahead, faintly irritated by Pete's interjection. He wanted to be the sole source of the cool thing.

'Yerman, DJ Space is playing,' he continued, to confirm his more intimate level of knowledge while also trying to appear nonchalant, 'at, mmm,' needlessly, he paused to check his Apple Watch, 'midnight, I think, and a few more of them lads, y'know, Death Monkey and DJ Horseflesh … It should be class, actually.' In spite of himself, Tom's eagerness was showing, and Kate realized then that that's what he'd been texting people about all evening, constantly checking his phone mid-conversation, as he was wont to do. He'd been planning to go there all along, had been waiting for the right opportunity to bring it up – or maybe he'd have preferred not to mention it, to go without the rest of them, to meet other 'cooler' people there after horsing up all of Pete's coke. *Fucking Tom, fucking disingenuous cock,* she thought, her inside voice almost spitting with disgust.

But then, Tom always wanted to go out raving. He actually had trouble with nights that turned solely into sessions. He'd had enough of them where he grew up, on that horse farm in Laois, with nothing for miles but fields and barns, not of the bucolic sort, but lined with muddy ditches and ugly wire fencing, with abandoned fridges in the hedgerows, and roadkill splattered all along the country lanes. He'd told a story once of heading out for a walk on his own one February afternoon and coming across three separate dead lambs, their little half-frozen, half-gnawed carcasses strewn across the fields like offerings. Back there, he'd had only vodka, ketamine and psychedelics to stem the silent, suffocating tide of boredom. Understandably, she supposed, he'd never stopped craving crowds, bustle, madness, city. He hadn't yet grown out of that demented student energy, and now, at thirty-two, perpetually single (due not to his height, as he supposed, but rather to his shit personality, although it was easier for him to blame the former), perpetually on the tear, maybe he never would.

he'd try to be funnier than the presenter and he'd insist on project managing. There'd be shots of him in a hard hat and hi-vis, holding up an architect's plan in the mud confusedly, completely out of his depth. And it would all go tits up, of course, his modern-yet-traditional blended bollocks of a mansion somewhere in Kildare or Meath, and then of course he'd have to throw a load more money at it just so it'd come all right in the end, or at least good enough for the cameras. Kate felt like she'd seen it already, could see his poor, slim, miserable wife, caked in make-up with the eyebrows freshly laminated and the lips done, with his arm firmly around her to stop her running off, sitting on their stiff, uncomfortable, blue velvet couch and telling yerman, the presenter, just how proud she was of her amazing husband, Tom, for pulling it off …

'Uhhh, I dunno, maybe I'll stay in, watch Marta myself …' she heard Joe say through the music of the *Grand Designs* credits. He was always reluctant to go anywhere these days, liking best the security of his own home, the proximity of his own toilet and bed. He had a girlfriend, a daughter, a good job, a PlayStation, and a cupboard with snacks – what exactly could a night out hold for him now? Everything he wanted was here, pretty much, so why ever leave?

'Oh Joe! *Jesus*!' Maria shot at him with another irritated flick of her hair, unwilling to have this conversation again, this slow coercion into motion of her ball and chain. Then, relenting slightly, not wanting to reveal her rage in front of the others, she cajoled: 'Iss your *birthday* Joe, less celebrate! And Kate is coming, righ' Kate? You'll come dancing, right?'

A pause. They were all looking her way – even Tom, who'd momentarily suspended his texting.

'Ummm,' she wavered.

Dancing, yes, she liked dancing, but *now*? Mostly, she wanted to just sit here all night and never move again. *Ever*. Preferably, to disappear into this spot, calcify, until the drugs were long out of her system and all of her life's ailments had been magically sorted for her, so she could wake up in a new, kinder, more successful version of her existence, filled with unifying love and meaningful friendships with people she genuinely liked, and small well-attended launches for her various novels and story collections, ones that served good wine and at which she looked positively glowing, rather than nervously sweaty. That'd be ideal. In painful contrast, the thought of having to move even an inch frightened her, because once she moved she'd have to keep moving, all the way to the end of her life; moving, going, leaving, arriving, walking, talking, eating, sleeping, doing, making, for ever and ever until death finally relieved her. And from her spot on the couch, paranoid and depleted, none of it looked worth the effort.

Ugh, but if experience had taught her anything, it was that she would have to move eventually, no matter what. She always did.

Unless she really did just give up and die, here and now? Although that would probably require some minor movement, in and of itself. A sort of slow slipping down, a thud onto the floor at the very least. At that moment, if she could have stayed completely still as she died, she might just have gone for it, but as it was …

'Mmm, I think I should probably …' She wanted to bow out gracefully but didn't know how to phrase it. She always found it so difficult to say she wanted to leave; it made her feel as though she was letting other people down, putting a dampener on a night. Her favourite way to go was to do so secretly, to silently gather up her things and let herself out, in the hope that nobody even noticed. Usually, though, like tonight, she left it too late, or was far too drunk or high to extricate herself stealthily.

'C'mon Kate,' said Joe, forcing a laugh, 'I'll go if you go … You can't abandon us now.'

'Yeah, c'mon, it'll be gas!' said Pete, doing his 'Oirish' voice with another enormous wink, because he was completely wrecked by now and could hold nothing back.

Kate was trying to sculpt her apologies, and she could already see her route through the city, could see herself projected into the near future, ambling happily down George's Street, arms swinging, and then turning off right by Hogan's, weaving her way deep through to Grafton Street, then up around by St Stephen's Green, on past the Shelbourne, peering in at the posh middle-aged people – the women in their poorly concealed Spanx under their too-expensive, unflatteringly tight dresses, the men in their brightly coloured shirts and corduroy slacks, all the big pink Irish faces, shouting and laughing and piling into private cars with drivers, onto the next spot – and then on around to the far corner, to Leeson Street, which she'd follow all the way along over the canal bridge and on out through Donnybrook, out alongside the whirr of cars past RTÉ, past UCD, before turning right, inland, towards Goatstown, back to her damp, crummy houseshare which, she hoped, would be empty. Her housemates were no doubt out on the tear themselves, were probably at the same rave this lot were going to, since they were of the same general milieu as these people here: late twenties/early thirties, with enough money to get themselves thoroughly fucked up of a weekend but not enough to afford a decent place to live.

It was just as she was forming this plan in her mind, enjoying the prospect of it, and thinking, too, about what music she would listen to as she flâneused her way along in her high-yet-peaceful dream state (*Anima* by Thom Yorke, probably, or *Music for Egon Schiele* by Rachel's), that she happened to glance down. There she noticed, with a surge of something akin to joy, but more metallic – a feeling at once pleasant and cold, blade-like – after having solemnly vowed not to watch it, that the place mat was lying on the table directly before her, with a big plump line on top. That might have been the biggest, plumpest line she'd ever seen, lying ever so patiently in wait for her.

'Yeah, sure, I'll come,' said Kate, already placing her drink down and angling herself forward towards the coffee table.

'Great,' said Joe, who was laughing now for no reason. 'Fuck it then. Let's dance.'

Gymnastics

She's in her late thirties to early forties, although she's been told she doesn't look a day over thirty-two. She has jet black hair and brown eyes and lips that make young men blush and inspect their feet when she catches them imagining. She's small and slim. She was in the 'A' strand of various teams in school: basketball, swimming, tennis, hockey, squash. But she was primarily a gymnast. She won a silver medal in the national under-sixteens' floor gymnastics competition. It took place on a Saturday in the capital, four hours away by car, in the gymnasium of a private school. One of the judges, a broad-nosed middle-aged woman, with spiky blonde hair and thick thighs under her tracksuit, placed the medal around her neck, and then raised her hand high for people to clap, as she stood, shivering with adrenaline, on the small wooden podium. The judge told her, leaning in under the inverted V of their arms, hands gripped tight, that she should keep it up; she was a natural. She remembers feeling the warmth of the woman's milky breath in her ear, which was pink and curved round into a narrowing funnel. She was fourteen.

She still remembers the routine, and directs the conversation, in beds with men, in the drowsy flow of half-formed words afterwards, so that they inevitably ask her to perform it for them. She puts up the required amount of resistance. She says, laughing dismissively, as they grope her beneath the sheets, trying to coax her open again, that it'll be no good, that she has practically forgotten it. She waits until the men are obliged to insist. Then she wriggles out from their arms, stretches on her bra, hooking it expertly at her spine, elbows crooked; threads varnished toenails through damp lacy knickers, and strides out; out into the garden, if there's still light, or new light milking through; the living room maybe; or a hotel's beige glowing hallway; the garage even; anywhere there's space, to show them.

She takes up the start position. She winks at the drowsy, tousled men, smiling as though to say 'God, I can't believe you're really making me do this!' Then she's serious. She takes each elbow in the opposite hand and pulls across her chest, twisting at the waist. She touches her toes, bending straight down from the hips. She's supple, for her age. She grabs each foot up behind and pulls back, leaning forward like a ballerina. She's cold in her underwear, nipples protruding under flimsy silk. But she doesn't notice.

She hasn't lost her figure, although without a bra her small breasts do droop a little, flat above the nipple and overfull below. The surface of her ass, too, is beginning to grow mottled. But only a little. It's still an enviable body. She takes care of herself. In the shower, she buffs her thighs with a scrubbing brush until her skin is red raw. She wears tight clothes in bed and avoids starchy carbohydrates. She still swims in the pool and plays tennis with her younger sister, who is quite good, in spite of the limp.

She conjures up the song for her routine, until she can hear it echoing around the gymnasium. She closes her eyes, counts herself in – four, three, two ... – breathes deep, hissing up through flared nostrils. Then, as the men light a cigarette, or check their phone, or try to call out a joke about not tripping, or as they shiver, annoyed at being forced to leave the bed (but mostly at being forgotten), she sets off.

The run in from the corner across the blue mat, light-toed steps, knees bent, folding straight into a double cartwheel, up, turn back, then down into a front flip, on into a tumble, up to a pivot around again, toes pointed out, arms graceful out to her sides. She has to be careful if the room or hall she is in has a low ceiling. She must alter the routine slightly, but she knows what to do. The performance lasts exactly six minutes, maybe six minutes and thirty seconds if it has been a few weeks. She is sweating and out of breath by the end, exhilarated. Her eyes gleam and her teeth are bared, and she is more alive, with just-discernible shudders ringing out in waves from the back of her neck down through all her white supple bones, flicking out her fingers like shooting spells.

The men clap, or holler, or say great, that was great, or you looked so sexy doing that. Maybe they look up from their phone and give a tight half smile. Mostly they hurry over to her, desperate to reassert possession; take her shoulders, or put their hands around her tiny, hot, moist waist, or push their groin against her ass from behind, lumpen, and say, so now can we go back to bed? Or maybe they say they have to get going. But it's not important what the men say or do.

What is important, she remembers, is to keep within the boundaries of the mat at all times. If she goes too far, if a toe slips over the edge, out of the designated performance area, points are deducted. It suggests, her trainer Mr Vincent told her after practice, repeatedly, in the frosty, white-tiled changing rooms behind the stage in the school's theatre-cum-sports hall, that she's out of control. It shows, he insisted, frowning down under dark caterpillar eyebrows into her eyes, that she's not the absolute master over her own body, her movements. And after all, he always said at the end, finally softening, reaching out towards her, that's the whole point of gymnastics.

Echolocations

I go to see a film of a woman in a garden. It's showing in the Irish Film Institute in Dublin. The garden is that of her childhood home in Cork. It's a mansion, really. Anglo-Irish pile, Georgian, that kind of thing. Or maybe it's neo classical, I can't remember. She has been away, in London, I think. It's her first time back. She's been gone long enough to idealize the place. Her body language is all chest thrust forth, *mummy and daddy* and *oh yes let's find where the old pony's buried.*

There's no one else there; she has arrived a day before the new staff are due to come, left to enjoy her reunion with the place alone. She's at that age when she is still foolish but thinks she has grown wise. She's probably around my age, I realize, appraising her – lines, hips, hair. Or maybe I'm thinking wishfully.

It's thick and lush, the garden. Wetly gleaming in the morning light. A stream passes blindly through it somewhere down below, away from the house. She rushes out the door and down the hill the moment she confirms that there's absolutely no one else there: all she can see are her old dolls, the curved staircase, the dusty attic, the tidy, disused kitchen.

As she descends into the depths of the garden in this film I attend one afternoon, she is channelled through narrow pathways between high hedges, around whose corners it's impossible to see. The foliage shimmers. She runs her hands over it, touches everything as she goes. The garden is planted with the usual; dark stiff yews higher up the hill, enormous green gunnera down by the water, beneath which moss and ferns froth lowly. The hedges themselves are of box and beech, the latter still half brown, turning half green, with a mixture of last and this year's leaves. Above her are shadowed black tress, overwatching like gods, through which can be seen patches of clear blue skies; an elephantine cypress with a low branch like a curved seat; a side-leaning larch; a few horse chestnuts, and a warty, twisted oak. It's all hers, the whole place. Green, more green, blue green, yellow green, pale green, rich green, and the too-bright white of light reflected against dew.

She is narrating her memories, a voice-over voiced, according to the opening credits, by an actress different to the one filmed walking. The voice enunciates in the Queen's English. This does not feel incongruous. Even as a child growing up in Cork, in that place, it's likely she would have that voice. Coming from the Big House, with grounds like these, she would have grown up both of that place, from that place, and not. She could probably impersonate a Cork accent, and no doubt did for laughs at school, or back in London. Hers would inevitably soften into a hybrid when she spoke to the servants the following day, or in the local village – her 'o' sounds broadening into a wind-beaten *aeh,* a few *sure*s and *thanks be to God*s thrown in where they don't, properly speaking, go.

The late forties, early fifties, it would have been, when this woman was growing up. A new time for her family: a time of transition – and transition precipitated by the external world is always experienced as a kind of loss. Perhaps they had all decided to leave, not just her. Perhaps, then, this film is not trying to suggest that anyone has died, that she is the only one left, but rather that she is the only one fool enough to come back. But why go back?

Something gone wrong for her in London, perhaps, the breakdown of a relationship, some dumb but suitably primed fellow with his own place in Kensington, who does something in banking and is a member of Hurlingham, from whom she'd been expecting a proposal any day now, for months, years, on end. All followed by champagne for one, then those last dregs of rum from the back of the cupboard, culminating in a series of indulgently suicidal phone calls. All as the moon, so sympathetic earlier in the night, gawped in at her through the tall, dirty windows of the flat.

I hadn't known what the film would be before collecting my ticket. It's one of those free lunchtime screenings, only half an hour long, chosen from the archive. I'd been waiting in a nearby coffee shop for a man I used to sleep with on and off many years ago, who hadn't turned up. Not even a text.

I am married now, as close to contented as my nature will allow. Therefore, I had been hoping with this meeting to convey this happy-adjacent state to him, this man whose initials I used to scratch along with my own into trees, desks, cubicle walls. This morning, before catching the train, I'd had my hair blow-dried. I'd worn impractical heeled boots and new, too-tight jeans that made my bum look like two ripe moons. *See?* I'd planned to convey to him, *I'm neither undesirable nor unhinged after all. Look how well I am. Look at how I've kept the weight off. Look at what your life could have been.*

I have escaped into the lunchtime screening to digest the new, sharp fact of his not bothering to turn up. It will provide just enough time for me to consume my own disappointment. At the very least, it'll offer a rest. Days out in Dublin – even those on which I don't hope to gloat across a coffee table from someone who used to orgasm at once within and without me – can be extremely tiring.

It is overstimulating for me, in that it often feels as though all the layers of memories I have of Dublin are humming and vying to be relived. Past selves, all those old, ill-dressed iterations, beat at the glass of my ears, jostling me into remembrance of things best left in the past; friendships lost, humiliations gained.

Dublin remains a velvet city, one that demands nostalgia, even of those who've never visited before. Overworn streets are made new and new again by minds and bodies growing older, over and over unto death, all as new bodies come to fill their still warm seats, to tell and listen in turn.

For me, it is always the same route; out the old bleeding side wound of Trinity by the empty gallery, pause for the *ding ding* of the Luas on the corner, across Nassau and up Dawson by the Hodges Figgis window, evoking the same thoughts each time a little more misremembered – 'but have you read his *A*? His *D* is very good.' Of how I'm as bad, how I always secretly felt there would be, should've been, for mine too: 'her *Green* isn't bad, but I think her *Blue* is better' – before turning right at Carluccio's, to stare in the window of the rare bookseller.

Erupting then into the overwhelm of Grafton Street, too busy, too bright, faces, memories – there I go with my mother down to have a coffee in Habitat before the

Christmas sales on Stephen's Day; and there I go rushing to keep up with my father, late for a film, late for the train, late for something; there drunk running for the night bus, crying or laughing over something.

Too much, too many; escape off quick again out the other side to peer passingly in the side windows of Bewley's, glance across to see the mystery of the angled church entrance, then back into the windows of the old jewellers, mercifully unchanged. Sparkle and shine, gleam and glare, and on along again, cobbled, to where – to where? – maybe over to George's Street and back around again, pass by the crowd outside Grogans who sit watching people watch them, right and then left onto Wicklow Street and in to admire the exotic, perfectly shaped fruit in Fallon & Byrne, on, onto where, Books Upstairs perhaps, and then to where, and again, and again.

And years will pass, and I will come back, and walk the same way, and breathe, until I, too, don't. And the last time will pass unbeknownst to me, and after it, the streets won't know I'm gone, they won't remember, and of my particular woven memories, my tread, nothing will be left in the city, not even whispers. No brown leaves will fall from me and clog up the gutters, nothing new to grow from my rot. No songs will be sung. And today, that day, this one, no one has come to meet me.

And yet, I am married now, with a house and a key that sticks and a particular breakfast I like eating in a particular way. I am a new, unexpected person in a new skin, a wife's skin. All that happened to me before this is now just that – things from before. They are not a part of this life. They have been left here somewhere, in Dublin.

No one told me and everyone did, of how, as I got older, life would become, in unexpected surges, desperately sad, even when it is happy, because of the accrual of memories of people and things irretrievably past. There's some niggling regret for what I've done and what was done to me, but mostly as I walk around the city, I experience both relief and a soft, permeating grief for all that pain now gone. Nothing shall ever feel as lusciously sharp again, I realize, as the romantic agony of my teens and twenties.

It is impossible to be in the same city twice. Although Dublin is a place in which plenty try. I see them everywhere, in old band t-shirts carrying guitars, or wrapped in tweed and oversized scarves. For these, time disperses on the air, slips out the cracked windows of pubs and cafés; it filters out with their breath on drunken dawns and out again with the yellow, rancid stream of their piss down back alleyways. Until one day there's a clean, bald pate where hair once thickly lustred; swollen blue veins rivering down calves; stiff, sore wrists and fingers. Damp now rises up the walls of the small flat that was once a temporary solution, perfect, they'd felt, for late night sessions and the swapping of joints and philosophies with beautiful, troubled women.

But the cinema is out of all that. The cinema offers a dark, warm hiding place, a place to absent the mind, to reset. It is still only lunchtime. There's much more day to come before home.

I live in a different city now, a train ride away, in my new, separate life, with my new, separate husband, who is not from Ireland at all, and knows Dublin only loosely. He sees it as just another city, neither historicized nor romanticized – touristy, over-monied, grasping falsely at a green and ginger-haired simulation of its past. I tell him of how it was before the money came and made it like everywhere else, and he listens patiently or talks of the same thing happening to his own home city, which makes me realize what a boring topic it is for the person who wasn't there.

It's just that, sometimes, my life now seems so completely cut off from the life I lived before that I can't remember what's real, and what is just some film I've seen once. I feel, occasionally, that I am waiting for this new warm, settled, pretend life to end, and to be told that now it's time to go back to the real one, the one in which Dublin is my city, its weathers my weather, its nights my night.

I am thirty-four, an age I never thought I'd be. But that only means I have accumulated thirty-four years of other ages, all of which brim and bubble within me, vying for attention. Now I am thirty-four, which means I am all at once newborn, six, sixteen, twenty-seven, and thirty-four. Sometimes even now, after all these years, I wake up in my bed beside my husband, and for a brief moment, I have absolutely no idea where I am or who he is.

In the lunchtime film, her path through the growth seems to grow narrower and narrower. There are large leaves that cast shadows, grasses that whisper and laugh. They move like people in crowds, swaying, dancing, leaning towards then suddenly away from her.

After a while, she comes to a locked gate. Through the gate is a man, rangy and unclean. This is the first other person we see in the film. Until then it has just been this actress (although there is, I suppose, the second actress too, the invisible one playing her inner monologue). He is clearly a workman.

Yes, there is a man, I remember that about the film; he is definitely there, but is he on the far side of the gate, or is he on this side? I can't recall. But I do remember that the gate can't be unlocked, that she is trapped, one way or the other, and that he – first seen, then, with a wave of dread, half remembered from before – is coming after her. She starts to run away, but he is a man, a native man, who has never left that place. There is no doubt that he will know its ways better than she ever could. He has worked it, still works it, by the looks of things. He has possibly been the one to plant those hedges, to lay the very paths she is trying to escape along. Or perhaps his father laid them, or his grandfather before him.

It's around this time that the mood of the film shifts. Although in truth, it has been unnerving all along, even when she's fondly remembering, flitting merrily from beloved nook to golden cranny. As she runs, something uncomfortably familiar runs cold fingers through me, and I shift in my seat. I am afraid for her. *Run!* I think, *run faster, you idiot, he's coming!*

Even though I know, of course, that this threat, whatever threat it is that this man embodies, has always been coming, and that it will get her in the end, whatever happens in the film. It has been there, latent, from the very beginning – it is the whole point, it's why they've made a film of her going back. They're telling us that this is both the draw and the danger of returning. It is, I'm told, what therapists often do with their patients – revisit, review, analyse past traumas. But then, therapists do it in sealed, quiet, private rooms, safely. As she runs, I curse the doomed image of her car pulling up on the gravel driveway, scorn her gormless glee of only a few minutes before, when she made her way up the steps and into the maw of the house.

Even as I sit there in the dark, I can feel it. Everywhere, the pulsing of what has been before: that is where we used to drink all together, twenty, thirty of us, there on those steps; and through that arch is where I used to rush from the train, forever in the rain, forever late for lectures; and that is where Bloom spoke to the lady about her mad husband, a riddle still unsolved, *U. P.: up*; and that is where Wilde liked to drink, apparently; and that's perhaps where Beckett threw up; and that could be claimed as precisely the spot where Countess Markievicz once choked on a nut – *or was it a legume?*

And there, in that building behind the advertisement hoarding that promises insurance for me and my loved ones against whatever might befall us, is no doubt where Oliver Cromwell contracted syphilis from some great-great-grandmother of mine (*no wonder he was so cross*); and that is where they stood up on the roof and declared a republic, somewhat prematurely; and there, under my fingers, are the marks where the bullets hit. And as I touch them again in my mind, I think of how many of those shooting were Irish soldiers in the British Army, just following orders, trying their best not to starve to death, and of how we prefer not to think of all that.

It is too complex, too much like real life, the makings of a poor story. History, from the grand narratives of a nation right down to our own, is better told like a fable. It must be made into something that can be lived by. History is either something one has overcome, or it is a better time filled with better people, to whom pints can be raised of a Friday night. In truth, if we could look through all of history in one small corner of any city, we'd likely see little but rivers of blood, tears and faeces.

The woman has managed to lose the man. For now, she's safe. But he is out there somewhere, and she must find refuge.

All the while, she's striving to remember and to not remember. Images come to the screen in flashes. A woman in a large bright kitchen, large-bosomed – a servant. A little girl enters. She is happy. She sits at the oversized table and is given something good to eat by the servant woman. It's clear from the blurry, vignetted shots and the voice-over that this is her. It is clear, too, that this is the safe place she's seeking, and yet we know, as she does, that this servant woman is long gone, probably dead, and besides, she is not a little girl any more. She is thirty-four, like me.

There are two other people in the cinema that afternoon. The first is an old man who sits in the front row. He is neat, in a blue rain jacket and red wool hat that he does not remove. The moment he sits down, he takes from his backpack a Tupperware box containing a sandwich and a flask, from which I can see steam rising against the darkened screen.

The other person is a curiously anomalous seventies-style biker dude, with long, knotted blonde hair, leather apparel, and that wide-kneed, slumped way of sitting that makes me want to kick things. Unlike the first, this man greatly affects my watching of the film, and probably my remembering of both it and the entire day now.

He comes in last of the three of us, just after the film has commenced, and chooses for his seat, out of all the empty seats, the back row where I am sitting, just one along from me. Coupled with some pointed, wide-eyed glancing my way, this seat choice suggests a deluded notion that there is a chance of this being a different kind of lunchtime experience. Some sort of *opportunity*.

In response, I turn my body away from him, recrossing my knees, and do my best to radiate disdain. All as she, the woman on screen, begins her frolic through the gardens. I am pretty good at radiating disdain, and he soon gets the picture. This is a relief, and I try to settle into the film. It has just begun in earnest; there she is now disappearing behind the pampas grass. I watch her as she pauses, looks up, and makes a hammy romance of surveying the verdant splendour, clasping her hands before her chest. Watching her closely, I am trying my best to ignore the man entirely, and have just begun to forget he's even there.

But wait, what's that? That sound? What could that be? I can't quite believe it, but when I look to the source, only one seat away from myself, I see that, yes, he really is, he's – *biting his nails.* I am horrified. I raise my eyebrows and open my mouth as I turn my head side to side slowly, conveying my utter amazement to the audience of nobody watching.

This, then, is the issue that arises for me, that afternoon in the cinema, after the man I used to sleep with has not turned up. All through the film the biker man proceeds to bite his nails, loudly. The noise is insufferable. It's a quiet film. *Snap, snap, snap* go his teeth as he works his way slowly and diligently around the curve of each one. Then he peers down from the screen at his handiwork, and starts in again on the nails of the other hand. He does this over and over again, until there can only be flittered, bloody nubbins left. He takes his time. He luxuriates in it. Picturing his nails, even as I force myself to watch the screen, makes my stomach lurch. Remembering now makes it lurch again.

I can't believe it. I can't fucking believe it. There she is, talking us through her memories of the old paths she played along as a child in her menacingly beautiful garden, and there he is, methodically biting his way through his thick, no doubt filthy, fingernails.

I turn my body back towards him to make a point of staring openly and noticeably in his direction, but now, of course, he affects to have no idea I'm there at all, despite his sitting so close to me that I could easily reach out and touch his knee. He simply cannot see me; I don't exist any more, as far as he's concerned. I clear my throat. Nothing. I shift irritably. Nothing. I sigh loudly through my nose. Nothing. Finally, I am forced to openly acknowledge the terrible predicament in which he has placed me: I am trapped. I can't change seats. It's a small cinema, and the rows go all the way to the wall on the left. The aisle is to the right, and he is blocking my way. I can't move without pressing past those awful, outflung, leather-clad legs.

And then, in spite of my best effort not to think the thought now hissing inside my mind, I become acutely aware of how he, too, must know this. And I fear that perhaps this is what he wants, this quietly torturous position I now find myself in. I wonder if this is some sort of revenge, this nail-biting, this drawing out of my attention. Is he trying to coerce me into moving seats, so that I'll have to endure the humiliation of our bodies, however briefly, touching? Surely not ... But then, equally surely, no one past the age of twenty bites their nails for pleasure? In a cinema, loudly? But then *again*, I reason with myself – staring at him, praying he'll look back at me and, thus seeing himself seen, desist – he does have that hair, and wear those clothes, and sit in that flopped-down, sulkily pubescent way, so what can I know of how he sees the world?

I shake my head, try to forget about him, to instead return to watching the film. It's the kitchen scene now, the recalling of the bosomed servant, the incomparable safety of other women for women and girls. I think of how the light that shines down in triangles through the high kitchen windows is beautiful, the room warm and inviting in browns and ochres. It makes me recall my own grandmother's kitchen in turn, how it overlooked the golf course edged in woodland, with the plum blue mountains beyond. And I think of how she too is dead. I think of how that house was sold, of how the new people had a second storey put on and got the kitchen redone, no doubt in marble of white or black, with a double-doored fridge and a kitchen island, although I bet they kept her old Belfast sink.

Snap, snap snap ... His nails, oh God. Fear, I feel it rise there in my chest, fear and rage intertwined. That old familiar. But what is there to be afraid of? Is this panic being caused by the film? I feel my breathing quicken along with hers on the screen, and I concentrate on slowing it down. *In-1-2-3, out-1-2-3, in-1-2-3, out-1-2-3* ...

Perhaps he is sitting there, too close to me, because he's completely unaware of his surroundings. Perhaps he didn't think about the seat he took and doesn't even notice that he's biting his nails loudly, or that it's bothering me. Or perhaps he comes to these viewings all the time, and I have sat in his favourite seat, and he has positioned himself there, too close, because it's the closest he can get to the seat itself. Or perhaps this whole thing is in my head. Were I to confront him, that's definitely what he'd tell me. That would be his natural, default defence. I can hear it already, playing out as it inevitably would: 'What? You think I ...? Holy shit, lady, you're fucking crazy. And anyway, you're not even hot!'

As I consider this imagined conversation, the humiliation I would feel (not that I would ever confront him anyway, that would be impossible), I glance over at him again. And it's then that I catch him watching me. And although I quickly look away from him towards the safety of the screen, immediately I know I have detected, or imagine I've detected – like hot, rancid oil seeping into my clothes – some little hint of triumph flicker across his eyes, there above the nails he still holds to his mouth, head twisting as he tears at them mercilessly.

The man in the film has reappeared, as we all knew he would. Now he seems to emerge from every corner, no matter where she flees. He clearly knows the garden too well. She is running again now. The sound of her heavy breathing, her feet thumping against the path, her frenzied thoughts, not quite willing to remember what she has so assiduously forgotten.

All is overlaid by the soul-destroying sound of the long-haired biker man's endless nail-biting. I cannot bear it, but I also can't get free, I can't get out past him. I will not. I will have strength, I will not run away, I will not 'make a scene'. I will not succumb to the ridiculousness – I can hardly bear to imagine it – of actually *leaving*. I'll do nothing, give him nothing. I'll wait patiently and quietly for the film to end.

Besides, why should I be the one to leave? To miss out? It would be unfair, another unfairness to add to all the others: not being able to travel to certain places without a man to accompany me, or to walk alone at night, or to fully forget myself in nature. Always this third eye, this watchfulness, this fear. But even if I could, I don't want to have to leave the film. The film is interesting, the film is evocative. I have every right to be here, in this seat. And it is only half an hour long, surely it'll be over soon anyway?

And there's also the fact that, if questioned, I would have no good reason to give for leaving. No one has touched me, no one has even spoken to me. Whatever I may have perceived, in truth, he's doing absolutely nothing. He's certainly not doing anything to me. No one, today, has done anything to me. That other one, he hasn't turned up, which is the definition of doing nothing. This one has, at most, sat too close. No crimes have been committed against me. Yes, okay, he's biting his nails loudly. But other than that, he's just watching a free lunchtime screening in the IFI. Same as the old guy eating his sandwich down front. Same as me.

I cross my arms and think of Dublin all around me, swelling and trembling in readiness, and I suddenly feel keen to be gone from the city altogether, to be away, back to my own, separate, adult life, out of the flow of all this remembering and reliving. I am not a woman on her own any more, however I may appear. I am not that girl, this one here, with all her glorious agonies. I think of home, of the place where home has become for me, it too ever-there, ever-passing, and a pang of joy runs through me.

But I must wait. I sit in the dark as the images glow and flicker, and I soothe myself by picturing my train ride home, pulling away, my face unknown to anybody. I picture the sea out the window, darkness falling, then the platform, the stairs, and there, my husband, waiting for me, in the bright lobby of the station.

He has her now, he has grabbed her in the dark cave of the bamboo grove. This has happened before, this is familiar – that is what we're supposed to understand. She has remembered too late. She should never have come here.

Well, duh, I think. She is now herself as an adult, now herself as a child. Some sort of terrible violence is recurring. But I am only half there. *Snap, snap, snap … Snap, snap, snap …*

The film ends. Without a moment's pause, the seventies biker nail-biter heaves himself up out of his seat, grabs his old, frayed backpack, and makes for the exit, head down. I sit and watch him go. He doesn't look up. Perhaps he doesn't dare.

After a moment, irrational relief coursing through me, I begin to stand, to look around myself in the newly lit room. I gather up my things: coat, bag, hat, gloves … The man below is doing the same. *Thwack* goes the catch on his lunchbox, closing again. The flask squeaks as he twists it tightly. I wonder if he is a widower, or just a lonely eccentric. I notice that he's getting his things in order faster than I am. Not wanting to be left there alone, I rush to leave at the same time he does, dragging my scarf behind me, coat only half buttoned.

As far as he's concerned, I think, taking the door he holds ajar for me, this has been a useful, warm way to eat his lunch in peace. After the brief interruption of the film, only half an hour long, he will continue on with his day: go see an exhibition, or meet someone, perhaps, for coffee, or dinner, or a drink – just the one – before getting the train or the bus home, to wherever it is that he lives. To his wife, or his husband, or his late husband or wife's ashes on the mantelpiece. Or to his elderly mother, or a sibling, or to the mewling cat. As will I. As will the other man, already gone. We will, all of us, go somewhere and sleep, and rise again, and sleep again and rise, and only perhaps, only ever in part, remember.

*

Walking down the long hall and emerging back out into daylight, I am momentarily dizzied, high and guileless on the winnowing out of stiff, sharp tension. I smile dopily as I stand blocking the doorway. A woman, around my age, taller than me, coughs irritably, and finally I move to the side, before slowly and without aim beginning my soft descent towards the river.

And there is The Ark, where years ago my own chubby face used to smile down from a windowpane, surrounded by other children. And here now is the river, where Viking boats came sailing in, came sailing in. And what about out the other way? Passing below bridges, 'sea air sours it', heard and – under she goes, and now, wait now, *there* – heard again. And now to where? Back into Dublin. Into Dublin, back. Even with all this rememorying, some things when gone are just gone, I think. All things, really, although it's easier not to know it. Nothing can be held. And perhaps that's why.

I wonder where the biker man is now, the tidy man who'd been sitting down front, my ex, my beautiful husband. All out there now, far and close, growing older. And even though it is too obvious to think, let alone to say, the thought rises: how there is only this living blindly forwards and remembering back, and that this dull fact is, in a nutshell, the tragedy of the thing. However it all turns out.

The Debutante

A woman moves to the capital to be with her partner. Even before she arrives she is running out of money, but she pretends she has found a job straight away, so that he won't disapprove of and ultimately leave her. She joins AA just for something to do (get out there, meet people!), and spends most of her days travelling to and from meetings all over the city. She doesn't share (what to say?), although it's true, she does drink secretly in the day sometimes, and the women in her family were all alcoholics.

On weekends she listens to jazz and drinks mixed drinks and does cocaine with her partner on a small oval mirror from the hall, always just a little too much (her, not him, of course), and they go out somewhere and pretend to be strangers picking one another up to go home and fuck, although this happens less now than when she first got there. Now when they fuck it is rare and if it happens at all it is usually after dinner or before dinner and he says 'I love you' as he comes on her stomach.

He has a proper job, and now that she's there and he thinks she does too, he wants them to start thinking about buying a place together (everything in the capital is a process with stages, which, she realizes, is just what proper life looks like – pre-consider, discuss, consider, discuss, co-consider, discuss, research, discuss, preliminary steps, discuss, decide, discuss, pre-act, discuss, act, discuss, complete action, discuss, admire, discuss, celebrate, discuss, briefly enjoy, discuss, find fault, discuss, worry, discuss, regret, discuss, fight, discuss, reconcile, discuss, pre-consider new object, discuss ...) – and so she plays along, even though she has no job and is getting ever closer to running out of money.

For her lunch she eats tasters in fancy supermarkets near the AA meetings, wandering the aisles and marvelling at the costs of things. People are so wealthy in the capital and they have so much stuff. Her partner is wealthy, his friends are wealthy, they all work even more than what she thought to be the correct, expected amount – all day, five days a week. Instead, they often work all day and all night on all the days of the week, which is exhausting and leaves no time for much else, but does make them quite excruciatingly wealthy. This allows them to buy life-enhancing teabags that cost six pounds per (small) box, one of which she steeps in hot water and drinks greedily every day, burning her mouth.

He is not a bad person, he is in fact a very good person. He finds something to be thankful for each day, be it a delicious lunch or glimpsing a beautiful sunset through the window of his office, or from a train. At the same time, he reminds himself that he is constantly moving towards a distant future; one that he can visualize clearly, like the end point of a very long run. She is envious of this, amazed, and so she must endeavour to be more like him, to participate, to concede, to defer, to *normalize*. There's nothing else for it – she knows where the other leads. She used to be mad. She used to see through inside eyes. Her tongue used to reach tasting all around the world and her skin used to be on fire. She used to balance on cliff edges, only half-hoping to be caught. She used to walk home alone at night. She used to fuck actual strangers, not just pretend. Once she was lost and now she is found.

She runs out of money. She loses weight. She is banned from eating tasters in or even stepping through the doors of certain fancy supermarkets. She stops going to AA, partly because she's heard it all before, and partly because, however hard she tries, she can think of nothing at all to say. Eventually, she is hit on by a man with expensive thick-rimmed spectacles standing outside a plush bar in the middle of an afternoon, a Tuesday maybe, and she is hungry, and she is desperate, and she remembers all of a sudden what it was to be mad, to be her unformed here-and-now self, and so she shrugs an inside sigh and yes, she sleeps with him for money.

She eats the ends of things. She begins fading around the edges. The skin around her fingernails is red raw and swollen. She's still there, her partner is searching for houses within their budget online, he is so happy to be taking this next step with her, he brings her flowers, and after he has left for work she eats the heads of them. She is there, she is just managing, then – 'poof!' – she disappears.

Shell

Before they married, Laura had been the type to pick off the brittle split ends of her hair one at a time and to throw up in bathrooms after meals she felt, retrospectively, undeserving of. She'd fucked anyone who held her gaze for more than six seconds, moaning and wailing and telling them how big they were – the biggest ever! Back then, she'd written free-form poems in her many colour-coded journals, sitting where she could be seen in the windows of cafés and dreaming of a time after her (imminent) death when they would be discovered and her genius, never recognized in her lifetime, would be mourned, most especially by all those gaze-holders she'd so briefly, loudly, fucked.

Then she met him and, unlike the others, he'd wanted to keep her. And so they married, one bright April morning between showers. And he took her back to his home – their home now, remember – and gave her champagne and oysters and pasta, soft and lacquered with butter, and when she tried to slip away to the bathroom after, he took her hand and said gently, lovingly, *no, no, no need for that*. He asked her *why, why do you, why would you,* and not knowing what to say exactly, not having ever thought before about the ideas he offered her – those of direct cause, of truth and lies, about blame apportioned or *generational trauma* – not having thought about anything, really, but instinct, animals, guts – out poured whatever she could think of, that might sound, to him, like a good enough excuse: oh, y'know, the usual, my mother, my father, my friends, my childhood … And all the while he held her hand tight and held her gaze tighter, six hours it felt, sixty maybe, or six-thousand-and-four, until her eyes were hot and red from staying open and she could come up with nothing else, her mind all squeezed out of words. And then when she was done he wiped a tear from his eye and said, *no more, no more of that now, I'm here, I'm going to take care of you now, I love you.*

Oh, she thought, okay. That sounds nice.

I love you too, she said. And, after a pause, thank you.

No, no, don't mention it, he said, although she could see that he was gratified.

When they had sex as man and wife it was a different thing to what she knew, *lovemaking,* he called it. There were a lot of whispered declarations interspersed with deep throaty kisses, and most important was making sure that she came first, preferably more than once, since, to him, she was all that mattered. It could be exhausting, but afterwards she felt very wanted, very loved, very seen, and thought for the first time in her life about how this wasn't just sex, it was how people made babies. How they would make babies probably, one day. Eventually.

Her hair and nails grew long and strong, like the hair and nails of women in films. Now, her nails were like how her grandmother's nails used to be, before she was dead in the ground (where perhaps they are still long and strong, and growing every day). She took to lying in bed most mornings, where he brought her breakfast and news from the world. It's sunny / raining / stormy out, did you hear the trees in the night? The man from down the lane was taken away in an ambulance this morning; the geese are back on the green; there was a dead mouse on the front step, must be a neighbour's cat.

And she lay back and spooned in her food and listened wide-eared as he rubbed her feet, telling all, and when she went to move he said, *no, no need, stay a while, relax, enjoy yourself – do you have everything you need? I'll call you for lunch, rest, you deserve it, after the life you've had.*

What treatment! She couldn't believe her luck! Her! After all those years in the wilderness! God, she thought, smushing herself down further into the eiderdown, if only they could see her now! If only they could see her!

Sometimes, her mother tried to call the house, or her father wrote, but she would be in bed, unable to reach the phone, or too tired to go through the rigmarole of reading an entire, whining, pleading letter. Away, away, she would deal with them later, when she wasn't so cossetted in comfort and bliss. They could wait, after all they'd done to her, remember? *Remember what you told me? I'm amazed they have the nerve, frankly …*

Until slowly, reluctantly, the ringing petered out, and she misplaced, or forgot, or perhaps he accidentally threw out the letters, the numbers she could call. An invasion into her newfound sanctuary by friends was something she didn't have to worry about – they'd never really liked her anyway, her selfishness, her tendency to lie, her unreliability, her manipulation and habit of finishing off their pints and boyfriends. Their silence only made him shake his head again in wonder, as he asked aloud how she managed to endure all that she had been through until now, the cruelty, the disregard – *they obviously never cared about you, did they?*

I don't know, you're right, I don't know how I did it, yes, that's true, if it hadn't been for you, my love, my knight in shining, no, I don't know where I would have ended …

Quickly, slowly, a routine calcified around her. Wake, ring the bell, breakfast brought. Stories, papers, books, and ne'er a need to leave the warm womb of bed until lunch, served downstairs, toast and tea and eggs to fortify her long, silken hair and ever-growing nails, after which, this far north, it was already dark – ah, too late! Whatever she had intended to do, too late for that now, try again tomorrow, time instead for dinner, for chocolate, for sleep!

She grew fat. Feeding her ripe slices of persimmon and pear, he told her she was beautiful, wonderful, that there was only more of her to love. She thought so too, it was wonderful, these sudden folds, her softness, her warmth. He rolled pearlescent lotion into the places she couldn't reach, and when they made love now, at least three times a week, it felt like being lost in an ocean, so hot and wet and rippling. He would bury his face in her so deeply that she couldn't see him, could only feel, and sometimes, in the privacy of her mind, her last alone place, she would picture, for kicks – although it did make her feel terribly guilty – one of the men she'd had before. Look at me now, she'd say, look how beautiful I've become, how big, how real, with her gleaming hair splayed out all across the pillows, the floor, sometimes spilling out the window; and her flesh, rolling like waves to shore, with every thrust of his tongue, this man who adored her, and she'd come, hard, thinking of those others as they watched and realized all that they'd missed out on.

Within a year of married life, the phone had stopped ringing altogether, letters never came, and she could no longer make it down the stairs. *But my love, what do you need to go downstairs for? Look, I can put a TV in here, all the channels, movies, and it is warmer and more comfortable to eat up here anyway. Here, look, I installed a bath in the corner while you were sleeping, and look, a surprise, behind this stunning, silk-printed Japanese screen I bought especially for you, a toilet – yes, solely for you, of course, my sweet, for your private business. I think, my darling, after everything you've endured, it is only right that I should get to take care of you, even, perhaps, to spoil you – although, if you don't like it, of course …*

There wasn't a precise day that she could remember, when she noticed that she'd lost her sight. Kept mostly in the dark as she was, swaddled so tightly, so carefully, in all this warm, honey-suckling love, she had lost need of her eyes long before. Perhaps, she thought at one point, maybe months later, maybe in her sleep, she had simply closed them, and forgotten how to open them again. It made no difference, she was so sleepy, so happy, so comfortable, what did she want with sight?

Nor could she tell, precisely, when her hands had disappeared, nor, later or before, her feet. They had sunk too deep into the fleshy realms of her centre, which no longer had much of a discernible beginning nor end, only folds and folds of softly lotioned layers, spilling out so beautifully it sometimes made her husband cry simply to behold her, *you put me in mind of a conch shell,* he told her, *you remember how conch shells look, do you recall them, darling? Ah, my love, if only you could see yourself as I do, you'd know I'm telling the truth when I say you are the most beautiful woman ever, to ever, for ever my …*

By the time two years were through (or, well, it could again have been six years, or sixty, for all she knew), she had become, from what she could gather, a shape that almost filled the room. There was just enough space for her husband to squeeze in the doorway (the actual door of which he'd long ago had to remove). Using a hard, wooden pole to push back the weight of her flesh, he was able to press himself along the walls. He would work his way around, grunting with the effort, until he found the window, which he needed for light, since her body had long before enveloped the overhead bulb. He would then press and roll her one way and then the other (*like stretching dough,* he told her, or, no longer having ears to hear, perhaps she'd only imagined that), until he found the appropriate hole, be it to feed, to kiss, to fuck, or to gently wipe, his beautiful, gorgeous, his delicate, broken wife.

Somewhere, close to her middle, where she could just discern, in the quiet dark of days or nights when he was off elsewhere (earning money, shopping, cleaning the house, preparing food, watching television, walking the dog, hosting guests), the faint beating of her heart or a rumble of digestion, she could also feel her long, strong nails, deep somewhere now, still growing, digging hard into the inside of her. But there was no way to tell him, and besides, the pain of them was nothing, compared to what she'd gone through before.

Now, she was so proud of herself, this woman, this loved and pampered woman, who used to get wet and cold at bus stops, who'd cried in pubs, who'd tried on tiny dresses in changing rooms, who'd counted out change at the supermarket till, who'd spent the whole night with lipstick on her teeth, who'd cursed the blur of condensation when she'd sat in café windows in the hope of being spotted. She, who for so long had been forced to endure the agony of existing in the world.

An Fear Marbh

This is based on the true story of a family – a mother, father and 'two to three children' – who lived alone on Inis Tuaisceart, the northernmost island of the Blaskets. The storm, and what followed, occurred in or around 1948.

It happened about four times in a year that there'd be a whole day with not a breath of wind on the island. Just before the storm that became the end, one of those days had come. But this time, the last time, the memories such days brought – with their clearness, their sweetness, full of the scents of lives that were and could have been – made the whole thing too much. There was the old fern damp of the well that made sore and cool the inside of her nostrils; the thick overripe of fallen apples; the fresh whisper of meadowsweet and montbretia on the roadsides in late summer; the warm, heady rot of hay in the old horse shed. On days like this, on the other, populated Blasket, An Blascaod Mór, the people would go on sprees, forget the work and drink and be merry. They would dance in pairs as someone pressed and pulled a music box across their laps, or threw out some notes in rings on a fiddle held below the ribs. 'Níl ann ach lá dár saol,' they'd say, rubbing their tongues through the many gaps in their teeth. 'It's nothing but a day of our lives.'

But there was no such fun on their island, and so there, the wind was better. The wind was where Sadhbh had come to live. The wind was the whistle and the roar she knew, the blasting of her skirts and the whipping of her shawl, the slices of sea spray against her cheeks and her eyes that even now, after so many years, were stuck permanently in that Blasket squint. These were the conditions of the life she had been given by God. Or so said the man she called her husband, who had chosen this island for them.

Afterwards, in the briefly calm times in the institution, when she could sit still without lashing out, or howling, or snapping off bloodily her fingernails with scraping at the walls, her children were brought in. Her own mother, undergoing hellish agitations in turn, always waited in the hall. She found she was unable to look at this creature that had once been her daughter – the flushed, pink, unfurling daughter whom she'd cast out for her sin.

On these days, when her children trooped reluctantly into the room marked 'Sadhbh Cain' at the urgings of the nurse, she was quiet. She hid her face from them, even as they in turn pressed their gaze against anything but her. This cowering form, they only partially comprehended, was the person once their mother, back on the island where they'd all tried and failed to live through the storm that wouldn't end.

Rather, they studied the room; the single bed, made in white, the cross nailed to the wall. Rooms, built up and across at right angles and covered over with colours, white and blue, were still a novelty to these children. Windows were the greatest marvel. It was always on the glare of windows where their eyes alighted in the end. Light and almost no wind, all the light and only, at most, a tiny hiss of wind around the edges of their frames. These were magic things, almost frightening. Where they lived now, back in Dunquin with their grandmother, they would rise quiet in the night and stand by the one in their bedroom and look out on the blue world. They would see who could stand the longest, the breeze from the wooden frame brushing coolly against their fingers like a mother's breath. Before long, terror rushed them all in a flurry of silent motion back into their beds: one for the boys, seventeen and fifteen, and another for the girl, fourteen, an arm's length away across the narrow room.

Their fascination with windows entertained and perturbed the village's adults all at once. There was something divilish in their staring. Too old they were, surely, for such wonderment and nonsense. But then, they reminded themselves, the puer craters had never before seen one. Even so, an irritation as well as a strange horror rose in them, the men and women of the village, when they spotted the finger stains left behind on old Mrs O'Shaughnessy's panes, from all the rubbing and pawing. 'God bless us and keep us,' they'd say, shaking their heads, but their eyes, in glances to one another, would be saying other things.

Their grandmother, too, was frightened by these bizarre obsessions, and crossed herself furiously when she observed them. The children were so animated and breathless in their amazement over the littlest things, they would rock and coo and tear at the most unlikely nothings, and end up fighting over them and howling. She almost feared they'd start foaming at the mouths; from the windows, to the patterned china cups in the cabinet, to the stove, to the gilded cover on the Bible, to an old, knobbled thimble, which had long ago lost its gleam. In truth, she knew, they were half feral. They ate too fast and greedily, with great heaving breaths. They pissed on the ground whenever and wherever the urge took them, sometimes even in the flower beds that surrounded the house, or on the graves of the churchyard before mass. It was quite a shock to see the girl, surrounded by friends and neighbours, hitch her skirts that first time on the dirt road before Kruger's bar, and squat, the warm liquid spraying out against her ankles and running in little mud-flecked rivulets back down the hill.

And yet, no one could deny they knew their scripture. They had the catechisms better than any of the village children, could reel them off by heart. Whatever they were, their grandmother was determined to swallow her uneasiness and to love them fiercely. She protected them from all scorn. She would not make the same mistakes again. To be unkind, or to judge, or to ever send them off to some rock in the sea to live a cursed life with a mad man. She didn't scold them for staring, for pawing and fondling, but rather told them gently to treat the glass with caution, not to touch it so much, as it was delicate, precious, could easily break.

Delicate, precious, could easily break. They whispered the things they were told under their breaths in their room at night, over and over again, making sense; like a spider's web, they thought. Or a witch's spell. Or a prayer. Or a mother. Maybe, they thought but never said, if they'd had windows like these back on the island, a way to let the light in and the darkness out, things might have gone differently.

Only the faintest wisps of white drifted on high, and the water lay still and gleaming all around in the sun's blind light, all the way to the mainland; and the few chickens pecking at the dirt, and the rabbits out nibbling in all directions across the grassy cnocs and furrows; and no sound but the circling seagulls and the distant bleating of the sheep being loaded by the men from An Blascaod Mór down below, to be taken back to Beiginis for the coming winter. They would not bother coming up to rest a while with the family – her husband, the man she called her husband, didn't welcome company of any kind, was rude and gruff and ungenerous, and besides, they knew well that she had no food to give them.

There was that time, many years ago, at least ten years if not more, when the priest had come with the professor, the first and last visitors, and she had been forced to send the eldest boy out to catch some rabbits, and they'd had to sit and wait for so long, too long, until finally he came back, breathless and muddy and shamefaced, his eyes hanging low, with only one small coney caught, and that not worth the eating.

The agony Sadhbh had felt, seeing them off, the rumbling of their stomachs audible above their protestations that it didn't matter at all, not at all, at all, sure weren't they full already from the big feed they were after having on the mainland that morning? Politely, they waved away her apologies, her pained concerns. So distraught was she by being unable to feed them, and by the sullen rudeness of the man she called her husband, that she didn't dare ask after her mother, to whom they might have offered to pass on a message – God forbid, Sadhbh thought, the old woman ever came to know of this, of how her daughter lived.

Watching them leave, down the hill to the cliff face, where they would have to descend backwards, slowly, carefully, shown the footholds between the eruptions of pink thrift by the boy, she'd felt her heart bursting violently inside her with the want, the *please take me with you* screaming out to their shadows across the air. Seven years they'd been there, then. And they were not even halfway through.

The roof of their dwelling, where they lived for those seventeen and a half years, built in ancient times, was half underground and covered over by a circle of heavy stones. She couldn't believe it when they first arrived. She was just beginning to show, her ankles felt heavy and swollen from the cramped boat, her lower back aching from the climb. He was apparently delighted by the sight of it.

'It's perfect!' he'd exclaimed, circling round. Carefully, he climbed onto the structure's roof, going slow to test its strength. When it proved solid, he smiled, and shouted again, 'this is perfect!'

She'd never seen him so happy, she thought, watching him. Then she realized, with a start, that she'd never seen him happy at all. Lustful, yes, thoughtful, yes, serious, solemn, satisfied, yes – but happy? The stretch of his grin unnerved her, and it took all her resolve not to turn her eyes away from him.

'You're not expecting me to live here, are you?' she thought of asking. But even back then, so early on, she knew not to say anything. Silence was what he wanted from her, silence and submission. And maybe if she gave him what he wanted, she reasoned, he would one day agree to take her back to the real world and marry her, like normal people.

She pictured, after a summer of this, rowing back across the water to live in a house a few villages away from their own. And slowly, over time, when she had proved that she could live a good, Christian, God-fearing life, her mother would forgive her, and all would be well again. And they would sit by the fire, the baby on its grandmother's knee, and they would gossip and coo, and it would be as though nothing so terrible as this had ever happened. To her mind, this time was her punishment for her sin – this barren island, his strange whims – and that was fair enough, because she deserved it. And so she would take it all gracefully, with due penitence, and she would be rewarded.

'Must be a thousand years old at least, more,' he said, musing. Still on the roof, he removed the capstone from the very top of the hovel and looked down into its bowels: 'we can place the fire in the middle here.'

'Hm,' she'd replied, picking at a sprig of sea campion growing from the low wall to her left. He grimaced slightly, not looking at her. Standing tall, swaying a moment as he caught his balance, he slowly carried the heavy, flat, round stone down to where she stood. Quietly enraged by her indifference, he said sharply, nodding at the low side entrance, 'the inside'll need cleaning before nightfall, it'll be covered in sheep shit.' And with that, without a touch of her arm or even a glance, he walked straight past her back down the hill towards the cliff, to collect their few provisions from where the boat had left them on the rocks below.

A storm came soon after the day of the priest's visit too – it arrived two days later, although it was not as bad as the one that brought the end, the one they didn't get through. Back then, all of them waiting for the boy to return with the rabbits, her husband had sat there meanly, saying nothing, which of course had made her more voluble, giddily foolish in her chatter, to compensate. He was still scowling when she ducked back inside after they were gone. He was made resentful by this reminder of the world, the notice she had given it, and worst of all, her betrayed longing to be a part of it. If he'd had his way, they would not have let the priest inside at all, the professor neither. What good were they to them, to him, her, and their children, who knew all they needed of the world, and who spoke to God more directly than that old sinner ever would, with his fat belly and his laughter, here on their very own holy island?

The eldest boy, who had caught only the one rabbit, was almost a man himself these ten years later, although he was still childish in his isolation and his innocence. On that clear, still day, he'd been sent down to the men loading the sheep, to collect the flour and milk and butter, in return for the rabbits and the eggs. He would come up that evening wide-eyed and overwhelmed, as he always did from the rare activity of men, so full of the strange red dawn of life beyond the family, to which he was only exposed once every few months for the loading and unloading of the sheep. Their wide, loose gestures, unheeding of low ceilings or delicate walls; the little paper sticks, filled with a stinking brown hay, that they put between their lips and smoked; their smutty jokes, and their stories of the sea and land as living things, filled with fickle fears, desires, magic. They were the ones who told him that this island, the island where he and his family lived, looked like a dead man from the mainland, and that this was what they called it – not Inis Tuaisceart, the north island, as he knew it, but 'An Fear Marbh'. They told him of curses and spells and horrors that circled all around them, that were in the air right now, even if he couldn't see them, that were all too terrible to imagine.

When he went back to their dwelling, he whispered it all to his brother and sister. These were things they didn't hear about from their father and mother. Although, somehow, they weren't unexpected, these things they were told. Secrets in the air, terrors and threats. There was something in the undercurrents of the family's silences, and certain moods of their mother's, that provided the children with a prior knowledge of them all. Everything they heard of the world and its horrors amazed them. Yet what was amazing wasn't their existence, but rather to hear them openly spoken of. For them, these horrors were like food eaten by their mother while they had lain curled in her womb, all of it both known and unknown to them, all at once.

Over time, the eldest boy's dreams became wild, and sometimes he awoke screaming silently, his mouth agape and his eyes wet and fearful. Sometimes, he woke up standing with his bare toes hooked over the edge of the cliff. Lately, he had often been woken by a pleasant caress that ran through his limbs and ended with a wetness in his trousers. Of all this, he spoke to no one, not even his siblings – although, of course, they knew. Life was lived mostly without need of words amongst this gathering of five separately pressing souls; father, mother, sister and two brothers, together alone on Inis Tuaisceart.

It was too quiet, Sadhbh often thought, watching her children anxiously. They knew no noise but the whistling of the wind. They had calloused, blackened feet, from the wildness of their living, and a stooped way of walking caused by the lowness of their home. Sometimes, they appeared to her more like animals than people. But then, she, too, was forgetting how to be. When she thought of the people she had known back in the old life on the mainland, they appeared to her strange, filled with sounds and customs that had become as alien to her as they must be to the tethered horse or the watchful hare. She couldn't begin to fathom her children's unknowable thoughts, nor the content of their whispers. But it was hard, with no music, and sometimes no light in the evenings but that given off from the few pieces of turf or, when that ran out, the sheep dung they burned in its stead, to play or tell stories. Not that he allowed any of that when he was near anyway, unless they were stories of God from the Bible, and those she was always getting wrong, mixing them in her mind with the ones her mother told.

'Mary never saw a fairy, it was an *angel*,' he'd correct her, his voice bitter with quiet rage. Or 'there were no hawthorn trees in the desert with Moses, woman, nor houses to bring their branches into.' In the end, exasperated, he forbade her from storytelling at all, and duly took over their religious education. He told her, spitting out the words, that she couldn't be trusted with their souls. In a way, she took this intervention as a blessing. For, in spite of his meanness with them, the harsh, quick slaps he gave them when they faltered over the recitation of this verse or that commandment, if not for that one hour a day of study, he might never have talked with the children at all. And besides, she was beginning to realize that he was right – their souls weren't safe with her.

They had lived there, yes, it really had been, it had been seventeen years and more. Almost eighteen, although by now she had lost count of the months and could judge by season alone. And every time she entered her own home, she had been forced to bend, and to stay crouched as she moved around, cleaning and gathering, and serving out the bit of food. She could only have straightened up at the highest point, right in the middle. But, of course, she couldn't stand and stretch herself there, for that was where the fire burned, sending up acrid smoke around the belly of the black pot that hung heavy with water, on up out the hole he'd made upon first arriving.

That hole whistled piteously in the storm, filling the circled stone dwelling with howling and humming and moaning. It became a kind of music to them all, one she could still hear, would hear forever now. The music of her demon soul. Now, heard in her memory, the sound of it intermingled with the occasional wails of other voices, interred in other rooms, and was disturbed only by the squeak of nurses' shoes as they walked up and down the hall.

He was not a cruel man. No, cruel wasn't the way she'd have described him, had there been anyone to describe him to. But he was certainly strict. Ascetic, she might have called him, had she known the word. He sometimes claimed God as his measure, his source of reasoning, but oftentimes, as she had very slowly come to understand, it was mere fancies of his own. He was visited by ideas for rules that seemed to appear from nowhere. They were like tiny, white-winged moths who whistled on the wind down through the ceiling hole, into the curl of his ear and laid their eggs in the soft flesh of his brain. Because nowhere, as far as she could remember, was it written that God wanted absolute silence, or fasting for whole weeks on end, so that the small bit of food they had rotted into seething blackness. Nor did God hate music, hate her singing as she worked, nor surely would He have forbidden her from asking the boatmen to bring a fiddle the next time they came, to entertain the children. Nor, she came to believe, did God require for salvation, this life, this terrible existence, lived alone on an island, with not a bit of company. For if He did, wouldn't everyone alive be living in sin but them?

Her own mother was a sinless woman if ever she knew one, yet she loved to be gadding about, seeing neighbours, talking up a storm. According to him, she would burn in hell, as would his own parents. He often said his older brother was already there, burning daily in a thousand hot fires. He told her, in detail, repeatedly, of how his beautiful blue eyes would be, that very moment, melting out, and how they would then be put back in, only to be melted out again, over and over for all eternity. He told her of how demons would be eating away his brother's flesh, his organs and his genitals, and how he would be stretched on the rack and have boiling water poured into his open mouth, and various other tortures she couldn't bear to recall. She had some vague memory of this brother from childhood, a handsome boy, with black hair like his and piercing blue eyes, and a smile that could be caught even at a great distance. He had died a teenager, this brother, an accident during harvest time, just the two of them out in the field, working late into the dusk, a time when it grew all too easy to make mistakes. Or so it had been said.

Of course, had she dared, Sadhbh could have said to him, 'you have sinned too. These children are yours, too, remember, and we are not married. I have seen your face clenched tight in the moment of weakness, there close above my own. I have heard your breath rasping in the dark. And so don't forget I know that you are flesh and bone, with needs, just as I am.' But she would never say such a thing to him. Even the thinking of such words put fear into her, in case he should read them in her eyes. If he knew the things she thought, she knew he would likely kill her.

But then, it was she who did it in the end, wasn't it? That was a funny thought, after all her years of fearing. It had been so simple. She'd wanted to find the source. She'd wanted, finally, to find the God of which he'd so often spoken, the voice of God, lodged somewhere inside him, that had told him to bring them here. She'd felt that, maybe, if she could talk to Him directly, maybe she could ask Him to let them go. Let them leave that place, the storm, the darkness, the sound and fury. She wanted to go home. She had waited long enough. She had been penitent long enough. Finally, she knew she could do no more.

So, she'd taken the familiar worn wood handle of his axe in her calloused hands, the one they used sometimes to chop up the wood from wrecked boats that got lodged in the rocks around the island, and she'd walked, crouched low, to where he slept. And she got down on her knees. And she smiled. She smiled because she was excited, now, for the solace she was soon to find. The hole in the roof sung its howling song above her as she swung the blade up above her head, and then, after a sharp intake of breath, followed its weight down into the splitting pressure of his black, lumpen form. Her loose, matted hair flew forward, and with a flick of her neck she whipped it back again. The blade, lodged, was hoisted out, raised, and again brought down upon him. His deep, guttural scream mingled with the storm, his voice blending seamlessly – even, she later thought, beautifully – with all the other sounds. She could never say this now, of course, but it was stunning, really, looking back. The glory of it, with God there, palpably there, circling round and through them all.

'Amen!' she shouted, laughing, every time she brought it down. *Thwup!* and up, and, *Thwup!* and up, and *Thwup!* and up again. Her arms forgot to grow tired. It was a frenzy of pleasure, of exaltation. Up and down she went, in and out, deeper and deeper without pause. Never in her life had she felt so strong, so free, so wildly excited. Hitting bone, it stuck fast, and she had to wrestle it out, before, laughing, she brought it down again. *Thwup!* 'Amen! Ha!' … *Thwup!* 'Amen! Ha ha!' She'd forgotten all about the children, cowering so close that, had she leaned back on her heels, she could have reached out and touched them. The music was so beautiful, she felt like she was dancing, and it was so invigorating, the glistening red spray, hot and metallic on her face, splattered across her dress, that it brought a faint memory of colour back into her world after all that grey, swirling weather.

It was when each piece had finally been separated, one from the other – legs from trunk, arms from trunk, head – that she finally rested her axe on the dirt floor to her side, wet now, stained, and crouched right down, and began her search in earnest. With her ringless fingers, her probing tongue, she burrowed through his wounds. Where would He be? God? He must be in there, he had told her that God was in there, talking to him, laying out this life for them. If she had to use her teeth, or tear him into strips with her bare hands, it didn't matter. She was going to find Him.

No, there was no denying, or so Sadhbh felt now, that had the day of perfect quietude not landed upon her so unexpectedly, making her so softly, so exquisitely alive again; with the two younger children playing in their silent way among the walls and the ancient gravestones that surrounded their dwelling place; and the eldest lingering down by the water with the men; and her, sitting out on the big rock, sunning her face, with all that time to dream dangerously back to those earliest dances of her girlhood in the hall in Dingle, or to the heat of her mother's fireside. Or, later, back to walking the lane home at night, lit only by the moon, smoothing her skirt and fixing her hair after those brief trysts with him down under the old stone bridge. An odd young man he was, she did recognize that even then, from that strange, inward-turned family, the mother still in black over the brother after all the years, forever besotted with her grief.

He'd been known amongst the village boys and girls to be reticent or, more accurately, resolutely unwilling to speak. So it had been a shock when he'd approached her that time in the dance hall and asked for her hand. A low, gravelly voice, so raw from disuse he'd had to clear his throat. She'd felt honoured. Slowly, as they'd begun meeting more and more, just the two of them, out on their walks through the damp fields or later under that bridge (for he had never, after the first time, deigned to go dancing again – he had come only that once, he said, and then only to find her), she had discovered that his mind was filled with strange, melodious things. The visions he began to share with her were full of violence and passion, absolute ideals. His talk was like nothing she'd ever heard. Here was no idle chatter about the harvest, local scandals, nor those overworn opinions on politics, all the usual dull guff of the fucking Brits or independence or wars coming across the sea from Europe, that all had so little to do with her. Soon, she could hardly get him to pause, he talked so seriously and so constantly in the woven patterns of his own intricate dreamings, all to do somehow with God, with truth and purpose and original sin. Only when he was kissing her, touching her, pulling up her dress, did he briefly cease his breathless talking.

Perhaps, Sadhbh thought later, she wouldn't have let him down there at all, so peculiar was he, had it not been for his beautiful face. The most gorgeous-looking fella for miles around, there was no denying, even her mother had grudgingly admitted it. His brother had been the handsomest of them, it was generally agreed, perhaps the handsomest ever in the parish. But after the accident, there was only him. To his credit, to the very end, he had remained bewilderingly beautiful – the kind of face that, seen unexpectedly, might trip a person walking. But there were other factors, too, at play. She'd thought herself no fool, and had not given herself as blindly as one might think. He was likely, or so it was said around the place back then, to inherit the farm, being the only one left. It was a nice farm, right on the edge of the village, with good, rich soil. The house was larger than most, and his parents were bent and prematurely aged with their mourning, and so, she thought hopefully, soon to die. And she, after all, was the sole daughter of a poor widow, not exactly a catch, and too thin, and plain of face, she knew, however hard she pinched her cheeks and bit her lips, to bring the blood up to them. She'd thought she had him sussed, was convinced she could see how it would go. And so, she let him in. Given a thousand years, she would never have guessed about this: about God's word, the island.

Those six weeks of sound came on so suddenly after all that still remembering. They arrived with one large thunder crack like God's whip across the sky, and before they knew it, the sea was churning and booming on every side. It was so hard, the hardest they'd known. The few chickens were blown away down the cliff before they'd had the chance to gather them in, while the rabbits, their only meat in winter, hid away in their burrows, unreachable. There had been barely enough dung to burn for the fire, and the wind and rain coming down made it hiss and smoke, choking them. And no light, no light, there seemed to be not even the faintest glimmer left in the sky for them. For six weeks it lasted, before the sky cleared and the sound ceased, leaving only sore eyes, and a ringing in the ears. The very day after it cleared, the men from An Blascaod Mór came to check on them, and found what she had done.

They would go to the islands, he said, holding her too tight around the shoulders under the bridge on the night she told him no blood had come again. She had not expected such a response from her mother, she'd thought there'd be an understanding, a complicity. But that was not how it had gone. 'Shame you've brought on me, on your father's memory … A whore for a daughter … Never again, in this house …' The words seared her heart like a cattle brand. Now he was saying that they would find an island all for themselves and make a life there. A new place, untainted, for them alone.

He had been surprisingly calm, as though he'd already known, had been ready for such news. They would go and make a new beginning, and it would be difficult, but it would be beautiful and, most importantly, it would be for God. That was what he told her. There, they would be king and queen. There, in their special, separate world, the child in her belly could one day run free, untouched by the ugliness of all this, by these people and their smallness, their rumours and temptations.

And she, Sadhbh O'Shaughnessy, as she was then, that young, plain girl sitting there, fourteen and three months, with breasts flat and pinched like field mushrooms, with downy hair on her forearms and a baby the size of a walnut growing in her womb – she could do nothing but be thankful that he wanted her at all. That was a blessing, she'd told herself, squeezing back the too-tight grip of his hand. The island, his disregard for marriage, as well as for all the good, traditional things she'd always hoped for – a big farm of her own, with music, talk, a wide hearth to warm her toes – well, their loss could be endured, for now at least, if it only meant he wouldn't leave her. Because he could have walked away. From all the gossip and stories she'd ever heard about men and women and their goings on, she knew he was more likely to leave than to stick by her. Yes, she'd hoped they'd marry, but she'd always known the risks involved, too. Yet here he was, telling fervent tales of their future. Relief seeped into her chest like honey from an upturned jar and, for a moment, she was almost happy.

There was no love between them, but perhaps that too would grow, once they were alone on their island. Looking back now, through the hole in the roof of her own circling squall, fingertips bandaged in gauze, the cross nailed there to the wall, she saw in fleeting visions how the choice of accompanying him to that place was only a way of putting off what was always going to be her fate. It was the choice Sadhbh would have faced, whomever she'd agreed to dance with that night, whatever kind of life they'd offered; that of a passing something before the nothing's void; of lying out on a rock on a calm day, face turned up to the sun, before the coming storm.

To Cure a Body

For her ache, she discovered a cure. It was simple, and comparatively pain-free. It worked on a basic principle – that a dull pain is negated by an acute one. To provide an explanation: a person wouldn't mourn athlete's foot, when faced with a sudden, vicious stab wound to the throat. That's the beauty of piercing agony – the pure white sheen that overwhelms the clutter and mud of other, less immediate ills.

Her ache was felt chiefly in the lower stomach. Some referred to it as 'heartache', but for her, this was anatomically inaccurate, even absurd. For her, it was located, specifically, in the pit of her womb. (She had not even known before that she could feel her womb, lurking there inside.) The ache wrapped itself around her fallopian tubes and enveloped her ovaries, making them blueblack-inky-feeling. Her womb's fleshy inner walls were turned to ash from the grief of it.

To give a sense of the time before the cure: she had developed an odour that she was largely unaware of. It was not dissimilar to that found at the entrance of underground train stations at night in summer – heat and engine oil and sweat and animal and piss and sex rising, with a hint of rose eau de toilette. Before the cure, her skin had faded pink and grey; vague, hard-to-see colours, blanching meek in between the real ones. She had trouble being. Clawing, gnawing, gnashing – these had been the words for her then.

Before discovering her cure, she had lain awake at night, unable to sleep, because of the dry heat, curling in the corners of her. She hadn't slept for months. Years, even. She'd lain clasping at air and soiled sheets, bunched in fists across the surface of the bed. Her insides had hissed and screeched at her like damp winter logs burning, until she'd felt that she'd sooner go deaf than suffer the sheer endless wall of it. (Of course though, had anyone been there listening, under the bed or lurking outside the bedroom door, they wouldn't have heard a sound.)

At this time, it would have been a relief for her to end. She couldn't pretend she hadn't dreamt of it, hadn't savoured the taste. She'd imagined it to be like diving head first into cool waters. Those electric blueberry-jelly waters photographed in catalogues, flicked through idly, while waiting around indoors for nothing in particular on muggy midweek afternoons. She'd imagined ending then to be like a floating outward, in the belly of that water, into nothing, in contact with Nothing. Forgetting the feeling of her body wrapped around her.

But now for a good part: she'd always liked to cook. And to eat! Even more than was necessary. She would have listed insatiability as one of her many defining faults. As a result, in her lingering confinement, she grew fat. A protective thickening of the flesh. Dulling layers swelled across her bones and thoughts. Food fooled her, momentarily, into believing that she was becoming full. Filled. (Similar to the ephemeral satisfaction of another tongue in the mouth, seeking strange, warm spit. Or semen burrowing in, warming the tummy.) Eating afforded her a vague respite, if not yet a cure.

Upon the eve of her discovery, had anyone decided, on a whim, to check in on her, they'd have found her chopping onions by the kitchen sink. The sink faced a window covered in a thin film of grime. The light outside signified day ending. She was making a tomato sauce with Italian sausage and rich egg pasta, and was going to eat it all up with warmed blood red wine. Soft liquid food to – for a second, maybe – quench the dry ash of her womb. She diced her onions finely, and their odour combined with hers, creating a savoury haze. The slight movements in the atmosphere around her eddied cinders and fumes. The oil was warming in the pan. The radio played, some song about living, and she listened vacantly through the din of herself.

It was in this absent, ocean-floor state, chopping steadily, that she managed to bring the knife swiftly and expertly down upon the very base of the index finger on her left hand (the one holding the back of the onion in place), severing it from the rest of her body. This was a surprise. Hot ash air escaped her mouth in a sharp rush, only to be sucked in again, quickly, between clenched-jaw teeth. She dropped the knife on the countertop. The sudden clatter was unpleasant. Blood spurted from the twitching finger, and her brand-spanking-new, fingerless stump. The blood felt exposed – it had not expected to be revealed to the world at this moment. It had been coursing happily through hidden tunnels and passageways, murmuring and giggling. Now it came in limp rhythmic waves, an unenthused ejaculate, shamed, the blushing crimson shocking in its vibrancy against the dusky evening light.

The radio played on – another song, something about love, or death. The oil began to emit a faint blue smoke. Impending fire. *Too hot, careful!* She turned off the gas with her remaining five-fingered hand. She paused. The room hung suspended. Blood trickled down her wrist over her elbow, soaking into the cuff of her dress. She knew it must be wet and warm, but she felt –

Nothing.

For as long as her memory was willing to unfurl, she'd known her ache. Now, without warning, there was only numbness – that long-sought void. The realization flitted behind her eyes. But she didn't blink. Her lip didn't even twitch. She was careful not to openly acknowledge, to betray. Not even on the inside of her mind. Someone would see. The ache would see. She knew she needed to conceal the thought from herself, to keep in check this quickening of her heart. To steady now. She breathed through her nose, slowly, deliberately. She waited for the room to settle.

A little aside, a recollection of the world going on around her: at this exact moment, as she stood there, suspended, studying the remaining parts of the hand raised before her face, a cat-shaped blur leaped up onto the windowsill outside, and peered in with yellow orbeyes. It had been attracted from the hedgerow's depths, perhaps by curiosity, or the scent of blood, or perhaps a conscientious awareness of the need, at this point, for a witness. It mewed, feigned a yawn, sleek pink-armoured mouth circling wide, and watched.

Without a word, without even a flicker across her long pink-grey face, she quickly, asidedly – as though her thoughts were busy elsewhere, on tomorrow's chores maybe, or the tomorrow after's – bandaged up her loss.

She used iodine and white porous cloth from the dusty first-aid kit, which sat atop the pine dresser that stood against the beiging wall to the right of the sink. (Note that the shelves of this dresser held no framed photographs, although there was plenty of space for them.)

She took up the knife. She didn't wipe off what had recently been her blood before resuming her dicing. The severed finger, now turning a fashionable off-white – 'Severed Digit Pallor' – lay untouched to the left of her onion shards. The browning blood had trickled in a small pool across the grooves of the board, dyeing the layers of onion skin a fleshy pink. Its metallic odour mixed well with the onion's warm, wholesome one. She didn't mention to herself what she was doing. The part of her mind in control of doing actions and the part of her mind in charge of taking note of those doings were not in contact with one another just then. She had cut the line. It was easier that way. At this moment, she simply was. A pleasant numb of Nothing. She didn't rush.

She reignited the gas flame, and tipped onion shards into sizzling virgin oil. They sloshed and hissed in the pan as she stirred. Their ruddy flavour rose to her nostrils.

The cat-shaped blur watched. It was black and well fed, with a red collar and a small silver name tag, but without a bell (for warning birds). The blur sniffed, reaching nose forward, before recoiling, compressing its body back in feigned indifference. It turned its head to the left and squinted its eyes closed.

She added crushed garlic and chopped tomatoes and a little squeeze of lemon, black pepper, salt and a few basil leaves. She added one teaspoon of granulated sugar. And still there was Nothing. The radio – yet another song, something about people and loneliness – continued to evince no reaction from her, although the sounds proved useful for distraction.

But she did realize, deep down somewhere in the quiet places, behind the radio, the hum and sizzle of the ingredients coalescing into soft red in the pot, and her busily clanking mind, that she could hear it, clearly. The absence. There was no screech, no hiss, no groan, no grinding flesh and bone. Anyone who entered her, at that moment, would have found inside only an echoing silence.

The sauce bubbled and reduced and thickened. With surprisingly little difficulty (considering her recent disfigurement), she opened the wine bottle that had been warming by the furnace, and drank deeply from the glass. The tannins slicked the inside of her mouth and throat with blackberries and spice; a thin blood-like film. Her pasta water was simmering and her usual place at the table was set. She lit a long, thin white candle with a match, flicking the flame against the box with a sharp twitch of her wrist. Then, the finishing touch: she took out the sweet Italian sausage from the fridge, and smacked the packet onto the bloody chopping board. Her finger lay dead and unburied, slightly to the left. She had not actively remembered nor for one moment forgotten it.

She took her sausages, and cut them lengthways down the middle. She then cut them crossways several times, to create small chunks. She threw the pieces into the bubbling sauce. Next, as though it were just a nothing, not pausing at all in the flow of her motions, she took the finger – cool, like an old man's cheek – and expertly slit it down the middle, from the fingertip to the amputated end. She put down her knife, and neatly removed the chipped nail from its bed, before gently tugging the long thin bone, the small rounded knuckles delicate and white, out from the centre. It came away easier than she'd expected. When she had divided it into two halves, running the silver tip of the blade along with careful precision – it was an elegant finger, she could appreciate that now – she chopped the flesh up crossways into neat little chunks, and, with a swish of the knife, scraped them down off the board and into the pot.

Now, how to convey the following ...

It was the greatest meal of her entire life.

It was intoxicating.

When her plate was finished, she piled it up again, and again, until every last scrap was devoured and she'd licked it sparkling clean. Halfway through, insatiable, she opened another red with a pop, arm flung back, and drank straight from the bottle, whacking it down on the table between gulps and smacking her lips together contentedly. She ate with such furious intent that she lost her breath. Sauce spilled down her chin and onto her chest, embedding itself in little caking dollops on her dress and trickling down her décolletage into the rift between her breasts.

She had forgotten a person could feel like this. Her eyes dilated and her body grew supple and soft and willing. Her meat, cooked to perfection, was melting in the mouth. With each bite, she felt stronger. She wanted all of it, thick and red, and she swallowed it all, deep down into her belly. It flooded through her trunk and limbs, heating her from the inside out so that steam rose off her skin, making it glow wet burgundy, like the skins of fat men in saunas. Afterwards, she took the pot into her open lap, legs spread, and ran her remaining fingers around the inside, noisily sucking the last of the sauce off the tips. Her palms and crotch and behind her knees grew sodden.

The combined odour emanating from her and her food became overwhelming. The air was dense with the heat and stench of it.

She felt, by the end, like she wanted to tip over the table and set the house on fire and fly screaming naked down the street, eyes ablaze. Sitting there, intoxicated and full at the kitchen table, belly bulging forward, she laughed in the face of her ache. It was really gone, she thought. She laughed, and laughed again, her head back, a guttural rupture booming from the depths of her.

At this point, the story can only provide a sense of things. Of the time after her discovery of the cure: she visited friends. She dined out. She chatted with her mother uninhibitedly, even, occasionally, giggling. She polished the hall mirror, she vacuumed the stairs and behind the couch, and her skin had never looked so good. She must have been using new products, they said, because her hair achieved a sleekness previously undreamt of. She bought patterned clothes from high-street shops and pungent, organic cheeses from farmers' markets. She caught the eyes of men who wondered what it might be like to sleep with her, and she smiled coquettishly at them, knowing. She wore purple, and brushed her teeth twice a day, every day. She was so ravishingly engaging, that not one person noticed her missing finger. It was so trivial, a nothing, compared to what she had gained.

She was the embodiment of femininity. Her womb glowed a radiant gold that blinded the women around her and made them secretly jealous. They wondered what her trick was. She was ripe and fresh and fertile, ready for plucking. People said it was a miracle. (Although they'd told her time would do it. They'd told her that time would cure her.)

The respite lasted approximately three months. Without her knowing, an ink-stained pearl of history and memory, an embryo too small to be seen by the naked eye, was creating itself from internal whispers almost too quiet for her to hear, and attaching itself, surreptitiously, to the renewed, viscous walls of her womb.

She went to plays by up-and-coming playwrights and tried oysters and laughed at comedy. She read Shakespeare's sonnets on trains, sighing, and had wonderful sex on a picnic rug on a beach with a gentle, cooing poet from Pamplona.

But something wasn't right. The pearl was growing, feeding itself on her throwaways, the things she would rather not have known. That comment her sister made; the drunk man at the bar, leering. After a while, her house grew vaguely musty, and she would find herself running out of clean underwear every now and then. There was hair in the shower drain, and she grew uneasy. Once, she awoke in the night, slightly restless. She tripped up in her heels while dancing. She developed cradle cap on her scalp, like a baby, and found herself scratching it on dates with quite charming men, so that the flakes of skin wafted down dreamily into her main courses.

Well. It's easy to guess what had happened. After those three months, she was back where she'd started. No; worse. Her body had developed a bluish-purple rash up her back which itched constantly, leaving blood and shreds of matter beneath her nails. Her eyes were sore, and at night there seeped a liquid from them that was thicker and milkier than water, which gathered in their inner corners, and which she found smeared across her cheek and pillowcase in the mornings. Her toenails were fraying at the edges, and there were red blotches on her thighs, where hairs refused to surface, burrowing instead back down into her skin. She grew desperate. She needed to be cured again. For longer. She resolved, hands rolled into tight fists (one with five fingers, one with four), to do whatever it took.

Now for the beginning of the end: this time, it took the lower half of her left arm, from the elbow. She made a roast, and feasted on it long into the night. She accompanied the meat with creamed potatoes and delicately steamed carrots and broccoli, dressed in lemon and butter. She flavoured the roast with rosemary and garlic and covered it in generous glugs of oil, to keep it tender. She cooked it at a low heat, for hours. The smell filled the entire street on which she lived, making her neighbours' mouths water with desire. She worked slowly, methodically.

This meal was greater even than the last. Tears escaped her, and she laughed, and sighed, and she felt that she understood the expressions that artists gave to saints in paintings. This time, the effects lasted a full year. Nobody noticed the missing limb. It was such a minor loss, for so great a gain. Time, they said. Time had healed her.

When the year was out, she barbecued a leg and ate it in the back garden with a chilled bottle of Sancerre and pretty flickering candles to keep the flies away. Later, she made a meatloaf using the tender minced flesh of her breasts.

Her meals kept her going for another four years. She learned to play bridge and developed a fondness for origami. Her father died in the spring of one year and she wore a black dress to the wake. People brought sandwiches of salted cucumber and ham and cheese with the crusts cut off, and told her over drinks that he had been a great man. She changed supermarkets, as she didn't like the customer service at her usual one and thought it was about time she did something about it. She accrued money and bought an opal necklace that was greatly admired by all who saw it, draped around her neck.

Finally, to tell the end – stories like hers must have an end: it was sunny outside, warm. The cat-shaped blur was lounging on the garden table, soaking it in. The cherry tree was blooming, and now and then it snowed down lazy white petals across the lawn, and small brown birds were flitting between it and the feeder hanging on the kitchen's outer wall. It looked like a picture taken for a classroom with the neatly written caption, 'SPRING'.

She saw none of this. The pearl of ache had returned, yet again, as she now knew it always would. ('Time', the great healer she'd been promised, seemed to have forsaken her.) She was busy inside, in the shadows, preparing yet again. The curtains were drawn, and from the outside, had anyone been passing, by foot or by car, they'd have thought that perhaps she was away, or had moved somewhere else for a while. Yet there was a stillness to the house that they'd have had trouble describing to others. It would have given them an unnerving sense of anticipation; of potential energy being held, momentarily, in check. The house would have seemed to them somehow disjointed; not fitting with the world marching on around it. It felt as it might feel to pop in, quietly, to check on a dozing infant, only to discover a gleaming kitchen knife, resting there alongside it in the cot.

By now, her skin had developed an oily, translucent quality. Her blue veins pulsed limply beneath her cheeks, and along the underside of her remaining wrist. What hair she had left, between the raw, blistered patches of scalp, was blanched grey and ratty. It could be found in pungent, damp clusters in dark corners all over the house, and in loose, thin strands across her clothes and bed sheets. Her lips had thinned to nothing, just more skin of face, caving in over small, stained teeth, with deep creases at each corner. They that had been so full! Her pupils, hard to detect under heavy lids, had become milky and dim. She found it difficult to see from them.

She placed her bathtub over the fireplace in the living room, and filled it with water. Then, she waited for the water to boil, standing with her silver-topped cane for support. She wore her silk white dressing gown, already dirtied at the hem. Wedging the top of the cane under the pit of her severed-from-the-elbow left arm, she used her right to drink the wine (dark red, almost black, and heavily oaked – a special one, she'd been saving it), and garnish the bathwater with thyme, rosemary, onions and garlic, thickly chopped carrots and celery, along with whatever else appetizing she could find in the kitchen presses. (She didn't want anything to go to waste.) There was a drunken recklessness to her movements now, lunging and weighted; to how she threw back the dusty bottle, spilling its contents down her front in staining rivulets; how she lurched from kitchen to living room, knocking against furniture and door frames; how she flung in her ingredients, splashing boiling hot water across the carpet, and herself, leaving small, steaming red welts on what remained of her skin.

What happened next seems inevitable, barely worth relaying. But here it is: when the bath was ready, the room was filled with a hot delicious steam so thick that, standing in the doorway, it would've been almost impossible to see her uneven pink-grey form emerge from under the dressing gown. If anyone had been there, and called out to stop her, she wouldn't have heard them anyway. (The ache was screaming in her now.) Anyone present would have only heard, too late, the muffled splash, the sharp intake of breath, as she lowered the last of her body into the boiling stew-water. They'd have been so confused about what was happening, that there's no way they could have dashed across the thickened, humid room in time to save her; to kick the bath from its perch and free her boiled, scorching flesh from cooking any further. They'd never have been able to discern, through the dense white wafts, or beneath the bubbling and swelling red skin, the expression of relief that graced her face. But it was there.

Meantimes

A girl with a side ponytail, red lipstick and a leopard-print jacket, sitting outside the canteen of the Barbican, taking a photo of the table while talking animatedly to the guy across from her. She puts her phone down, facing up. She bobs her head and chews and lifts her eyebrows up and down to emphasize her point. I've seen her through the large floor-to-ceiling windows from my booth tucked away in the corner against the far wall. It is, in colours and style, reminiscent of a mid-century public swimming pool; pale duck-egg blue leather seats and white tiles, stained yellow by the golden, halogen lightbulb hanging exposed from above.

I have seen this too:

My open journal, not offering the genius and insight I'd hoped to find there, no beginnings of some brilliant project, a future book that would matter, or make my name, whatever that means. I have seen, many times before, this laptop (secondhand, warm and humming with age), my empty glass and stained coffee cup, my pinkish, blue-veined, typing hands. And again. And again.

I'll tell you other things I've seen, in the meantimes:

I've seen the body of a Mexican man in white jeans lying on the side of the road, a gun resting not too far from his outflung hand. I've seen people gather round to stare, close but not too close, fearful, as people and animals always are, that the violence of his recent death may prove catching.

I've seen my mother's breasts, drooping into points as she dries her legs and feet after a bath; one foot on the closed lid of the toilet, towel down between each of the toes, around by the heel, then swapped over for the other.

I have seen the cast of *Friends* grow thinner (the women), fatter (the men), older and wearier. I've seen them do this again and again, on syndication. I've seen photo montages of the changing face of the one who died above the text outlining how it happened: of how apparently he was alone and on ketamine in his hot tub in the Hollywood Hills.

What else?

I've seen geese flying in formation. I've seen footage of tsunamis, both silent on the horizon and roaring and violent up close. I've seen Italian men expertly thrust pizzas into stone-built pizza ovens using a long wooden utensil with a flat, round part at the end. I've seen the sun rise above the mountains in Montenegro, and the spines of dolphins crest the sea in Killiney Bay. I've seen red-faced middle-aged people who've never read *Ulysses* dressed up in long skirts and boaters for Bloomsday. I've seen period blood turned dark on my tampons, period blood turned dark on my underwear, period blood bright red and freshly slicked on a penis. I've seen the tip of other strained, eager penises ejaculating directly into my face, and I've seen a vagina like a permanently flayed wound spurting liquid in an elegant arc into the mouth of a beardless man. I've seen the foundations of buildings being built, I've seen endless miles of graveyards stretching along freeways in the United States, I've seen Macaulay Culkin slap his face and scream, every year for years and years. I've seen people take medicine: placing pills daintily into their mouths with a thumb and forefinger, or tossing them in more roughly with their palms, followed by a sip of water, or in liquid form, on a spoon, with sugar, to make it go down. I've seen people tie tourniquets around their arms before sticking needles into the soft, baby flesh on the underside of their elbows. I've seen the inside of an elephant's womb. I've seen presidents address nations after and before catastrophes, from which place and time, they've solemnly assured me, things will never be the same. I've seen cities destroyed after bombs have hit, I've seen skylines bristling with slowly swaying cranes, the grey and metal spines of elevator shafts going in first. I've seen sheep graze on steep cliffs in rain, I've seen how you're supposed to light a fire in a fireplace, by building a little house of fuel and placing the matchstick's flame in the middle. I've seen a Black man fuck a white woman in an extremely clean kitchen, somewhere in California in the 1990s. I've seen men punch walls, and women snort cocaine from a proffered key in a tight bathroom cubicle. I've seen my hand going into and out of a giant bag of tortilla chips until there are no more. I've seen cracked bones burst forth from skin. I've seen roast meat being expertly carved, and I've seen roast meat being inexpertly carved. I've seen an aeroplane taking off, I've seen an aeroplane burst into flames, I've seen a lightsaber in action, I've seen Hannibal Lecter suck his teeth, I've seen the Eye of Sauron, and I've seen countless people killed by bullets and fistfights and swords. I've seen the slow, mesmerising progress of brown crabs shuffling along the ocean floor fathoms below where I stand, atop a concrete harbour in West Cork on a late summer's afternoon, before the band starts up. I've seen a homeless guy trying to sleep on a subway get jostled by irritated, busied commuters. I've seen another guy throw a half-eaten burger and chips and the packaging from the window of his car on a motorway. I've seen another guy look directly into the camera in a grey room somewhere in Romania as he tells me how all women want to be dominated. I've seen a baby being born, plenty of babies being born, and I've seen my grandmother's desperate, contorted face lax into fallow emptiness as she dies. I've seen how the clouds look when viewed from above, stretched pink and gold-tinged for miles and miles and miles. I've seen a single cumulus cloud against a blue sky from my seat outside a café below, thrumming still in upness. I've seen the making of *The Matrix* bonus feature on the DVD, Keanu Reeves being lifted in his harness, Harvey Weinstein smiling and slapping backs on his way to somewhere else. I've seen dirty clothes pile up in a laundry basket, and hairs in the drain. I've seen smoke rise from the bonnet of my car. I've seen couples receiving therapy for free on television talk about how much they hate each other but how they love each other too, and how anyway, there are the kids to consider. I've seen men in bars make the decision to go right on ahead and place their hand on my knee, or on my better-looking friend's knee instead. I've seen my own shit sitting in the toilet, unwilling to flush. I've seen swans do their courtship dance on a still lake. I've seen brown foam and a beer can and an old styrofoam takeaway box collected in the reeds by my feet as swans do their courtship dance on a still lake, and have then looked up to see a plane pass overhead. I've seen advertisements selling coffins in instalments, a certain amount per month over a certain amount of years. I've seen the swollen, starving bellies of African babies, flies landing unheeded on their large eyes as they look straight back at me. I've seen old and fresh scars on old and young wrists, a tattoo of a brain rising like smoke from a box, a tiger wrestling a snake, a stillborn baby's name and date of birth (and death) in florid cursive on a young man's neck. I've seen the chicken mush they use for chicken nuggets moving quickly across the screen on a conveyor belt. I've seen flurries of snow circling Westminster at dusk, I've seen inside the all-white minimalist pad Kim Kardashian once shared with Kanye West, and inside Kendall's room specially designed for art-making with her friends, filled with new, untouched easels and new, untouched paint brushes and paints. I've seen Dr Jennifer Melfi get raped in a stairwell. I've seen the Dalai Lama appear as a guest judge on Australian *MasterChef*, smiling benignly as the others give their pithy, camera-ready verdicts on the food. I've seen (and heard) a tree fall in a forest. I've seen friends go by the wayside. I've seen teenagers make love. I've seen a man expose himself to small children in a playground. I've seen a Chinese lady making hundreds of thousands of dumplings at lightning speed in the brightly lit window of a restaurant in Chinatown at night. I've seen bread fresh from my oven, taut fresh sheets, the sheen of freshly washed hair. I've seen a robin eat oats from my hand in a white, sharp winter somewhere high up in Killarney National Park. I've seen a sailboat afloat on water made almost invisible by the brightness of the light. I've seen the person I love laugh and cry and rage and vomit and come. I've seen his face asleep and have thought, 'he will look like this when he is dead'. I have seen photos of us both together, laughing, smiling, on beaches, and have thought of how we, along with everyone else alive, will soon be dead. I've seen all this and other things, and still have infinities more to see.

Land of Honey

The fermented tang of shit struck her nostrils as she woke again this morning. He had done it again. *He had done it again*. But how, when he hadn't eaten in so long? Nothing at all for the last few days but the few spoons of tinned tomatoes, and even those watered down. That was all either of them had eaten for almost a week. Eeked out, she'd been able to make one tin last two days between them, but they were finished now. Today, there would be nothing. This, then, this shit he was producing, was perhaps the last of food eaten years ago, all those long-gone meals: buttered garlic prawns in Spain, curries in India, bread and cheese in Paris, and all those roasts, every Sunday when he was home. The thought of them now made her nauseous, such excess, such hideous consumption. And now it seemed the last of all that was leaving him. The stench was so overwhelming she thought she might faint, the bitterness of it, in her nose, her throat, her emptily gaping and heaving stomach. It was coming from him, there, that man who had been, in her life, this one life, now soon ending, her husband. There he was now, still there in his chair, mired there, as he had been for weeks, across the cold, black hearth from her.

With a difficult jerk of her head, she shot her gaze up from his feet, to briefly take in the face of the man who'd released this acrid, burning smell, to which she'd yet again awoken with the first dawn light. She saw, as always, his head lolled forward, drool sinking down onto his tired, greying shirt. All about him was greying, now, even the light in this room appeared grey; the white walls were grey, the paintings, the carpet, the empty, stained plates and mugs, all overwashed with grey, as though a fog had stolen silently into the house and spread its stain across everything.

He slept, but his sleep, she could see, was fitful, fretted. He furrowed his brow, tried to lift his right arm from the chair's rest, a slight flex in what was left of the muscles. Too weak, he was of course too weak. The thwarted arm, stuck fast, desisted, the shirt's material laxed, and his expression softened back to sunken, becalmed dreaming. He was always dozing now, never fully awake. If he would just wake, just for a moment, she could ask him what she ought to do. They could make a plan – he might think of a way to call for help, to escape. But for weeks he had been in this half-living state, drifting only to a filmed under-surface of consciousness, never alive enough to speak with or even to recognize her. She had thought of setting the house on fire, but couldn't be sure that they would be noticed and saved before burning alive. And cold as she was, tired, desperate, hungry, lonely as she was, she couldn't face the prospect of burning alive. If they'd had a gas oven, she'd have found a way to let them both die by it, but the damned thing was electric. Not that she could have carried him to the kitchen. She too was growing weaker by the day. She tried to lift her own arm from its place, resting tucked down by her side, and felt a juddering, a slight movement, but that was all. But it was early yet, and she was always stiff in the mornings.

She would try again later. She would no doubt manage something later.

The house phone had long ago become disconnected, a wire down, she thought, in that last bad winter storm, and she had no idea where to find the charger for the one mobile phone they shared. She had, before her strength had left her, rifled through every cupboard, scraped down the back of both their wardrobes, stuck her gnarled fingers right to the back of the drawers of his desk, but to no avail. He had put it somewhere safe, long ago, and she had never thought to ask where, and now it couldn't be found, and he couldn't wake long enough to be asked, let alone to answer her. Now he only slept, and half-woke, eyes blurred, groaning, and took some water from her, some tea with no milk, or some of those watered-down lumps of tinned tomato. Before he had sipped the last spoonful he was asleep again; a panting, frowning sleep, the effort of swallowing having been almost too much for him. This left him impervious to questions, to pleas, to the tears she might have shed, could the energy for them be found. She had long since stopped trying, which meant she had long since stopped hoping.

These days, they lived in a world without words, voiceless, but for the rooks. They had taken to the small copse of swaying larch just beyond the overgrown, untended back lawn, in the small flat area before the low hills of the mountain began. The noise of them. If she ever got out of here, she would never forget their noise, the horror of their dusk screeching, their waking morning squawks.

The fridge, too, hummed still, breaking the totality of his and her silence. It was almost mocking, she sometimes felt, humming away happily to itself while they sat on. She knew every tone and note of it by heart. It would never have occurred to her to simply turn it off – the thought was too terrible, its implications, she could not allow it to rise in her mind. And water still sometimes gurgled through the walls.

It was also a painful truth that, every now and then, out on the road to the front, past the half acre of front lawn (which, being also untended, had turned to weeping brown and yellow mush), the bee's whirr of a car's engine, or the slow, rumbling trundle of a tractor, could be discerned passing up or down the lane. This was the worst sound, the most terrible one to hear. Life passing. Help, passing. There was no way to signal. The gate was locked fast against strangers, locked against anyone who might chance to come. He had always insisted on their locking it, while the house itself was obscured by yew hedges and holly trees. He'd planted them the first autumn after they'd moved here, a whole row of them, bare rooted but tall already. They would be ideal, he'd said, for the complete, uninterrupted privacy they sought. Privacy, then, had seemed the closest they could get to freedom. Freedom was not being bothered by anyone, by choosing the terms on which they were forced to meet with other people, with their problems, their worthy causes, their personal or political disasters, their inane conversations.

Oh, and there was the rain, of course. The rain was worse than their silence, the rain she dreaded. If only, if *only* she could have closed her eyes and ears against it. She felt it in her hands first, the pain shooting through them, and she knew the sound would soon follow. She waited, sick with anticipation, for the first cut of it to strike the glass. It could be interminable, an attack on every front, drumming on the windows, the walls, the doors, the roof of their bungalow. It invaded the house, coursing steadily in streams down the chimney of the hearth right by where they sat, pooling there, growing stagnant. She was becoming certain that it pooled too in the sunken centres of all those long-unvisited rooms – the dining room, the bedroom, the hall – pooled and grew, drop by drop. So enormous had the pools in these abandoned rooms grown, she was sure that, were she to open any of their doors, she would be struck down by a wave of water of such force that it would drown her in an instant, pour roaring out and engulf the whole house. Even if she could, she would never, now, try to open those doors, to visit those places; those dark, seething, flooded rooms. They were too dangerous. And so, little by little, as the rainwater whorled and rose blackly, her world had contracted, until now all she had left were these few spaces, this one, the kitchen, and the little toilet beyond the kitchen. Although, come to think of it, she hadn't been there in a while. How long? She would perhaps go check on them later, when she felt less tired. Hopefully they would not be flooding yet, they had held out this long, although she was constantly checking the lower walls for the first signs of damp, peering carefully at the floor tiles for treacherous slicks of liquid. There were hazards everywhere. Her years in this house, this land, had taught her that. Even the safest-seeming things contained secret dangers. Just look at them, just look at him and her! With their well-laid plans. Now, her life was a matter of avoidance. Maintenance and avoidance, a careful strategy of not thinking and not seeing. Her days were spent trying to shuffle as silently as she could between all of the myriad encroaching dooms. To remain small and insignificant and unnoticed, eyes to the floor, quiet as a woodlouse.

Mostly, it seemed to rain in the night. The sound of it woke her often, but sometimes it would rain all day, for days on end, rain like she had never seen, certainly never back in England. All the endless mud and rain and silence of this cursed place, this afflicted island where, she now knew, people came not to live, but to die. Why had no one told them? But then, who was there to warn them? They had only each other, she and her husband – that thing, sitting there, frowning again, murmuring something voicelessly to himself. He was the one who had always made the decisions. He was their leader. And now he couldn't be woken. Now it was too late. They were stuck here, glued to the spot, isolated even from one another, the air burning her eyes with the reek of his shit.

Perhaps, she thought, sitting there across from him, hating in a sudden surge his oblivious absence in sleep, his abandonment of her – perhaps they had never really been together. And so, perhaps – but the thought, it stung, it was too raw, too awful – it was always going to go like this, even had they died better, died warm and cared for, in a nursing home in England somewhere, or surrounded by the love of the children they'd never had. She could now see without wanting to, here from her vantage point, that whatever they might have done, it would always have been him over there, an infinite distance away, unknown and unknowable, and her here, contained, alone, destined to die as she'd been born: one small, whole, curled-up creature, afraid and crying unheard, as the world went on spinning wildly. Round and round and round it would go, as indifferent to her death – she now understood – as it had been to her life.

A jerking wake, as though someone had gripped hard her shoulder – what? What happened? She blinked, swallowed the thin scraping of saliva that stuck fast her tongue and palate. She opened her mouth. It was brighter now, light was coming, there, the wall, illuminated. She must have fallen back asleep. And – ah, she had forgotten, she gagged, coughed a dry nothing up, the smell, she had forgotten – it had grown worse, if anything, his stench. She closed her mouth tight again. Keeping her head down, she looked at his slippered feet, for signs of life, listened ... Yes, a breath, a slight shifting, another breath. He was there, still with her, still breathing. She noticed, then, attempting to take in a relieved lungful of air through her nostrils, and feeling the sharp dagger pain of another cough failing to release itself from her chest, that she herself was having difficulty breathing. Setting her jaw, she tried short breaths through her false teeth, rasping them out rhythmically. She tried to take in only the thinnest whisps, so as not to let this damp, cold, faecal air too far into her lungs. Her eyes took in her own hands and feet. Their warped shapes ached. These days, her body was nothing more than a sequence of messages, each one signifying distress.

In a quick, decisive movement, in spite of the sharp agony it caused her, she thrust her eyes up to look at his face again to see if he might be, finally, awake, might be there to contradict her, to tell her no, all's not lost, he's with her, has always been with her. His face had grown so old, so terribly old and thin, although to her it was just as it always had been. A husband's face is his face is his face, just as the sky's the sky or the sea the sea. And now, as she looked, holding her own ruined face aloft for as long as she could bear it, he opened his mouth slightly. She watched, mesmerized, as his dry, purplish tongue emerged slowly onto his lower lip. She thought he might be preparing to speak, and she felt the cold, shimmering beginnings of hope flutter through her. Then she saw the tongue retreat back and disappear, leaving the silence unbroken. Now, he appeared to want to shift the weight of his lolling, sleeping head over to the other side, no doubt to relieve the strain on his own bent neck. After a moment's barely perceptible struggle, in this, too, he failed, and so he stayed as he was, looking towards her lap through closed, unseeing eyes, a perturbed, unhappy expression drifting across his hollowed features. Unable to hold her head up any longer, her spine already hissing in agony, she too lowered her head to face back down into her lap. Her familiar hands and feet lay there still, curled and useless like foetuses in brine.

To remember that her body might ever have been a source of pleasure to her now seemed so ridiculous that she might, were thoughts of other states of being still available to her, have laughed at the idea. It was a container of pain. Her very bones and skin were the layered encasement within which she was trapped, hungry, sore, and from which she was unable to escape. It was pitiless, this body, that would not give her a moment's peace, and would not let her go. And his was no better, although at least he could sleep, could dream, forget this nightmare of the present, this unbelievable yet happening series of moments, of which only she was cursedly aware.

She still, even now, after weeks and months of this, years perhaps, couldn't quite believe that this undignified calamity was to be their end. It was idiotic, even strangely embarrassing, that they, two people who had lived fully in the world, were going to die like this, alone and forgotten, in a bungalow, on a lane, with neighbours out there right now, not too far away, moving around their farms and houses, watching TV and working and cooking meals; and beyond them, villages, towns, cities, all bustling with people, people who might help, if they could only be alerted.

They two, him and her, who had in fact lived better than most; they who had travelled the world, who'd made love like Hemingway on hillsides in Spain; who'd seen Greek tragedy performed in open-air theatres in Athens while sipping wine from plastic cups; who'd swum at midnight in the Pacific Ocean surrounded by the glow of phosphorescence, and who'd watched the Northern Lights from their lonely camp on the uppermost fjords of Norway. She and he, who had been so vital, who'd eschewed the trappings of friends, family ties, children, so that they could live for themselves, for each other alone – right to the end.

Not that she remembered any of it. She never thought, any more, to make comparisons between their lives then and now, or between that meagre, dying shape of man sitting there, and the one she had married. That vital young creature in uniform, glanced by her as she'd walked along the pier in Blyth one evening, standing and talking by the rails with some men, all of them measly, weak, ratty in comparison. They were like fish biting at his heels, those others, his inferiors. She walked alone, as she did every evening then. Her mother would, same as any other night, have taken to bed straight after dinner, with a book, a gin, and complaints of a headache. Always, the woman was sick – sick of her daughter, sick of her husband, sick of the demeaning drudgery of her perfectly ordinary life.

Her father would have been out in his little garage at the back, pretending to tinker with an engine and resenting any presence but the dog's, even that of his daughter. Out there he could enjoy the brief relief of solitude, the safety of the wireless that would talk away merrily and expect nothing of him, no answer that could be held up to the light, only to be scoffed at and repeated to make him feel stupid or belittled.

She didn't think he'd even noticed her passing, the dapper young man. He'd never stopped in his flow of speech, hadn't met her gaze when she dared to glance at him. He had seemed a man above noticing her, this girl, five years younger than himself, so small, plain, demurely dressed, her head, as always, lowered to her feet. To her, he had looked, in comparison, strong, slim, unspeakably beautiful. But then, in those days, she did have a tendency to fall in love with a different man almost every night. She sought them out on her walks, and would find a source of incomparable manly perfection on at least four out of seven nights a week. She would go home, and touch herself, not thinking of sex, but of romance, pleasuring herself with the thought of that night's suitor sweeping her off her feet, romancing her, buying her nice things – jewellery, dresses, a car, a home with a garden all her own, all the while whispering in her ear that he would always, always love her.

But this one, the one who would become her husband, he really had been special, she told herself afterwards – and not solely because he'd been the only one to ever speak to her. He'd been so commanding, even amongst his friends. She'd admired the way he held court, his hues, as she glanced at him, made up solely of healthy browns and glistening blues. He had just come from a three-month posting in the Caribbean, although she wouldn't find that out until the following night, when he walked her to the pictures. He'd been lonely there, in Jamaica, and sickened by the life he saw, which he described as one of lethargy and indolence. 'Lotus eaters', he'd called them, and she had nodded along wide-eyed, pretending to understand. Not for him, he told her, that sort of life. He wanted action, adventure, sights. Hard work, followed by well-earned pleasure. Most of all, he confessed, smiling a little at himself, he wanted a life of the mind. A worthy life. This, he told her, was what had attracted him to her – the book she was carrying that night.

She had, as always, grabbed a paperback from the hall shelves as she walked out the door, had taken it without even looking, because the cover, to her, appeared suitably intellectual. It was a new one of her mother's, that was all she'd known of it. *The Myth of Sisyphus*! He couldn't believe it – it was one of his favourites. Did she like it? Oh, well, she'd only just started reading it ... But yes, she did, she always brought a book out on her walks. Although of course she didn't tell him why. It wasn't that she didn't like to read, she did, but mostly she brought a book along so that, if the weather was nice, and she wished to idle a while, she could sit on a bench, and look suitably preoccupied, perhaps even mysteriously interesting, to any young man who might observe her. Apparently, the trick had worked. He did think her interesting, all because of this book. It was the book, not her person, that had made him follow after her.

Later that night, panicked and smitten, she'd sat up in bed until 3 a.m., trying to wrap her mind around it. Pushing a stone up a hill, over and over – what did it mean? She would need to figure it out, to understand, so that he would not discover her ignorance, and take his affection away from her. All she wanted, in those days, was to be loved. To have a man, any good man, who would adore her more than he had ever adored anyone else. It was all she had been taught to want, and believed, like every other girl she knew, that it was the best and most perfect thing to hope for.

From then on, she read with a seriousness she had not given the endeavour before. No longer did she read for romance and the excitement of the stories, but for ideas. She would not, she vowed, merely appear intellectual to him, she would *become* intellectual *for* him. (Only later, when that first bloom had faded, and she had begun to understand what marriage was, did she begin to read in earnest, for herself.)

No, she never thought of him now, that young, tanned stranger, the one who'd left his friends and hurried to catch up with her. She never did meet them, those other young men, nor did she ever meet any person he called a friend, all throughout their almost sixty years of marriage. He'd had acquaintances, men he played bridge or tennis with, or served with in the navy, but they weren't *friends*, and they were certainly never invited to the house. He had a brother, a much younger half-brother, she knew, but he didn't like to talk about him, or about his mother, or his father, who'd both died when he was very young. And so she'd never met this half-brother either, and had soon forgotten his name, let alone his whereabouts.

He'd caught up to her quickly, slightly breathless, and at the end of the pier, by the lighthouse where the van always parked, offered to buy her an ice cream. Cherry flavoured, for his cherry. A cheesy line, but she'd lapped it up, blushed demurely, just the right amount, exactly as they'd advised in the magazines. Once, having turned back, they reached again the very beginning of the pier, he'd asked if he could accompany her all the way home. Just as she'd so oft imagined a young man might. Her body blazed with the wondrousness of it, and she nodded a shy, smiling assent – again, just as she had practised. He stuck to the script she'd dreamt up perfectly, speaking of himself, asking her polite, leading, mildly flirtatious questions. It was as though, even then, he'd had some secret access to her mind; some little hole in her skull into which he could burrow silently like a tapeworm. That very first night, upon arriving at her house, he'd led her by the hand around the side passage, out of sight of the white-laced windows. Once there, grinning, wordless, he had pressed her back into the prickly, yielding mass of her mother's flowering escallonia and, lifting her skirt, touched her down there, his fingers finding her surprisingly unresisting. They were met only with a soft, warm supplicating wetness. His fingers were cold and rough and fumbling, yet to her they were divinity itself, and she gasped quietly and pressed her face into the material that covered his strong, tensed shoulder. When he finally took them from her, he brought them to his nose, and sniffed. Then, instinctively, he put them to her mouth, and she sucked, hard, right down to the knuckle. This made him gasp in turn, and he'd grabbed her close and shuddered hard against her with pleasure, burying his face down into her hair. She placed her hands on his lower back then, and held him there, soothing, in no rush, no rush at all. They had all night, all night. They had the rest of their lives.

Much later, in the first flush of their marriage, when all was wonderment, the story of finding one another was told over and over again, as it is with all young couples in love. He told her that when he'd first met her, she put him in mind of a hare he'd found once in the garden shed as a child. He'd discovered it trembling in the far corner, curled into as small a shape as possible, ears low, its face buried in the wall. As though, he said, musing, finishing the toast she'd brought him in bed, it thought that by refusing to see him, it in turn would avoid being seen.

One of those misapprehensions of early romance, or so she'd thought in the years that followed, remembering the hare, his image, laid so crudely over her. She had been nothing like a caught hare. If anything, she thought, she'd been more like a fox, pretending. The hare was nothing but evidence of the idea he'd wanted to have of her. A relic from a time when they'd still had the luxury of seeing the version of the other that they'd wanted to exist, rather than, as came later – as always comes later – being obliged to acknowledge the stark fact of who each really was.

They had moved to this house when she was fifty-nine, he sixty-four, some fifteen years earlier. She knew this, the information was there, somewhere, in a closed room of her mind, but she did not remember it now. Nor could she remember the sensation of pure delight she felt when she'd placed these chairs like this. If she were to recall it, the image would be accompanied by an unnerving pang, as though such a foreign feeling must even then have belonged to someone else, an interloper in her mind, someone who was never really her. She would have been forced to recognize that she didn't know that woman, the woman who positioned them. That maybe she never had. How could she not have seen that they would do nothing more than sit and die in these chairs? She should have run from them, or set them alight, while she still had the chance. She should have vowed never to sit, not ever, for anyone. She should have owned nothing, accumulated nothing, and then maybe, now, she would not be trapped here as she was, within the walls and seething wet grounds of her very own house.

Surely there must have been a shiver, a foreboding, that she perhaps, in her foolish rationality, her blind incomprehension of death, put down to nothing more than a breeze coming down the chimney. Just another nothing, another little nothing, like all those others that must be batted away in a life and a marriage. And had she really not seen the folly in bothering to whitewash these awful, cave-like, wattle-and-daub walls? Not recognized, deep down, the uselessness of placing that rug there, hanging those pictures just so? And there they hung still, seen by no one, not even her. Covered in dust, wrapped in that foggy greyness.

What was in them? Sea scenes; a Victorian ship silhouetted before a pink dusk; the red sail of a Galway hooker against various shades of greenish blue; low, crouched men pushing a currach out into water, brown capped and obscured by white flecks of salt spray. All nods to him, a seafaring man, his days in the navy. His glory years. The years about which he, in this green, quiet, private place, had intended to write great poetry.

From his thin, hunched form, the faint high hiss of wind escaping. This reminded her of the smell pervading her nostrils every moment – to think she could have forgotten it – and she coughed, the cough phlegmy and racking, sending darts of pain up her spine and into her brain. Then she too returned to a fitful sleep, in her own chair, just across from his.

They'd bought them together on holiday, at an auction just outside of Cashel years before, and had brought them across to England, to their home in Sunderland. There the two of them had sat in exactly the same positions, angled at forty-five degrees across from one another, hers on the right, his on the left. Only then, they were in the conservatory, that bright, clean, warm place, with a round table between them for the coffee. There was a rack below for the papers and magazines, and a view of their neat square of garden out beyond. Bulbs in spring, herbaceous perennials in summer and autumn and then, to get them through the winter, there was the sarcococca's heavily scented little white flowers, along with the fiery red of the dogwood stems and the spindly yellow clusters of the witch hazel. All through the warmer weather the copper beech used to cast pleasant drifting shadows across their pages as they read – or, she'd found it pleasant, at least. To him, that tree was perpetually growing too large, always encroaching, ruining the peace of his few free afternoons. Every year he made a fuss of having to cut it back, silent and thin-lipped and sweating profusely. All because she'd planted it one year without consulting him, when he'd been out at sea for three months with no contact whatsoever.

Until now, those years had been the worst of their marriage, and he'd convinced her, she later thought ruefully, that it had been the house, the situation, Sunderland, that was the problem. Sunderland, with its old, grey stone buildings and decaying, littered shipyards, its enormous Tesco and B&M car parks, its impoverished mothers smoking fags as they waited for buses with their children, and those overgrown graveyards that seemed to go on for miles and miles, filled with dockers and miners and boys blown to pieces in World War I. To him, the place had never felt far enough away from the centre of things to be truly wild, nor did it feel close enough to anywhere alive to receive vital heat.

Later, as she began, after the first good years, to hate this house, this country, its backwardness, its mistrust, its terrible health system and the closed worlds of its village communities, she began to pine for Sunderland. She realized that there had been nothing wrong with it, she had just been lonely. It wasn't the place itself, but rather her life in it, that had caused her pain. So much time alone, and that deep desire, not so much for him – although she did continue always to desire him, above all – but for anybody's company. She had always been bad at making friends. She'd never had a true friend but for him, and he'd never really been her friend. He'd always, from that first evening on the pier, been her big, strong man, her husband-leader. They were not the type of couple who considered themselves 'best friends', nor did they laugh that much together. Beyond books and the idea of a higher purpose, they didn't even have very much in common. Yet he would not have liked, she knew, to come home from sea, or even from an evening playing tennis (which, he insisted, he only bothered with for his health), to find her sitting at the table with a neighbour woman. Conversing with such people, he communicated without saying, would demean her, sully her intelligence. She was special, noble, beautiful of soul. She was the woman he had chosen for his wife, not because he liked her, but because she was the type of young woman happy to walk alone with only Camus under her arm for company. It would have cheapened her to him, to have a friend, to need other people.

She understood this implicitly. The idea was that he would stoically miss her from his place aboard ship, and she would with equal stoicism miss him here, and then they would, one day, come together again, a pure, unspoilt union of two, their love all the better for having been built on a mixture of total sacrifice and total dedication. And when they were together, off on their travels, living the life they'd envisioned, she was convinced he was right. She was committed to the idea, the whole world consisted of only them, and it was beautiful. His head between her thighs, she would be aroused to climax by thoughts of their spiritual purity. It was only when he left again, kissed goodbye at the door and then walked down the driveway and around the corner without ever looking back, that her resolve faltered.

Not that she managed to make friends, even when she weakened, and tried. In spite of all that early romanticizing, she had grown into a severe woman, odd in her habits. All parts of her, from her neatly clad feet, to the shape of her mouth, to the way she wore her hair scraped back from her face, had over the years come to convey an unyielding nature. Everything about her had become pulled tight. Only alone with him could she allow herself to reveal her malleable softness. This was because hers was a softness, as she was later very clearly made to realize, that she had offered up too readily that first night. Her supple willingness under his hands had made him not only want her, but distrust her too. He knew from that very moment that here was a flaw he would need to train out of her. Some part of him, what he considered to be the most traditionally romantic part, had been disgusted by her reciprocated desire, even as he fell in love with her. Although, naturally, all that only became clear long after they were married, and it was never actually said.

On the rare occasions she was invited into other women's kitchens, she was more like the hare he'd once wrongly imagined her to be. Alert, watchful, ever-ready to spring forth towards the sweet release of their front doors. She sat completely still, but that stillness contained a humming energy that could have powered a town for a week. It burned off her, and made the other women flush, and babble, and spill things. One dropped her good teapot. It smashed against the red, quarry-tiled floor, splashing shards of porcelain and hot tea all over both of them. Even when they managed to get as far as drinking the tea, she made the other women uneasy; what could they talk with her about? She wasn't remotely interested in their children, however sweet their singing voices or exceptional their achievements in maths. Never was she invited to tea twice, and only once did a woman take her up on her awkwardly proffered offer to visit her own home in turn. On that occasion, she was so fastidiously tidy when the poor woman, in a moment of forgetfulness, placed her teacup directly onto the table rather than the coaster, that she immediately picked it up and returned it to its correct position with disapprovingly pursed lips. Soon after, feigning a suddenly remembered appointment, the woman left, with none of the usual promises to return.

... How much time had passed? The square of light, she sensed, had moved across the wall; it was directly before her now. Oh God, she needed to piss. She needed to go quite desperately. She tried to stand. Her brain sent out its messages to her arms, her legs, her spine. But what was happening? Where were the responses to her command? Nowhere, nothing. Nothing was happening, her body was not, she was too weak, there was no – and then, before she even had time to think, it was coming, it was already – a shocking hot flow of wetness, oh no, oh God, she could feel it, burning as it seeped streaming, along the crack of her behind, into the seat beneath her, the once-beloved chair, spreading out across the undersides of her bony upper thighs. And as soon as it came, she realized that the feeling was familiar, that this had happened before. And the recognition of it was so sad to her, it made her feel so wholly desperate, that her mouth opened wide, a silent howl. Then, just as suddenly, she closed it, and fell back again into another fitful, restless sleep.

The screech of the rooks woke her. It had grown darker, and she became aware of the desperate cold. Her hands, her lap and feet, they were still just visible, but only their blurred outlines. It must be evening. And where was he? His feet, she looked, yes, could just make them out, still there. She held her breath, listened. A faint whistling inhalation. Was that his, though, or hers? No, it must have been his. She watched the feet. They were unmoving. But that meant nothing. He was only sleeping. He was always sleeping. Maybe someone would come, maybe someone would still come and rescue them. Tonight, or, perchance, tomorrow.

A gurgle of water in the walls. Black night had fallen – when? No moonlight penetrated, suggesting clouds. She listened. Little whispers of rain hit the window, teasing, cruel beginnings. *Oh please,* she thought, *no more rain, I can't take any more.* The house kept filling with it, the great flood. And as it rained, they were dying. *We are dying.* The thought came and was pressed away, *away away away.* She was so hungry, her stomach seemed to be adhering to itself, she could feel its walls pressing emptily against one another to form, no longer a bag, but a single, smooth sheet of dark red flesh.

Death had never been real to her before, not like this, not like now, now when it was truly coming, slipping this very moment through the cracks and around the doors.

Death was like all that water, seething, rippling soft and black in the unvisited rooms – she could almost hear it, churning, impatient, taste its dank rancid liquid coating the inside of her mouth. Or was that – the smell – his shit? She sniffed, waited. No, that seemed to be gone now. Where had it got to? She sniffed again. Had he woken, and gotten up, and cleaned himself? Was this all a dream then, this dying? Perhaps he was somewhere else right now, alive and well, in the kitchen, or the garden, or oh, she screamed silently in a small, gagging whimper, *oh! Don't go into those rooms! Don't open the doors, no, be careful, don't* – contorting her face in panic, she screwed her eyes tight and jerked her head upwards one last time. No, no, it was all right, he was there, still there, she could just make out, in the blackness, the familiarity, his shape, she was convinced he was there. He was still, must be still, asleep. The rain thickened, a gust of wind rattled it into the window behind her, and she shivered into the room's frozen motionlessness.

No one was coming. No one was coming. It was just a matter of time now, not much time. Only it was coming, it was coming for them, had been making its way to them for years and years. Ever since the moment they were born. She knew that now. She did. She thought it, and the glimmer of light it gave her mind made her recognize its truth. She tried to bat it away, but it would not leave. Death was coming now. Death was close. The terror expanded black in her chest, she could taste it, she really could taste the black water. She swallowed and felt it rushing down the outside of the flattened walls of her empty, red sheet stomach.

It wanted them both, him and her. It wanted their love for two, their ideal life. They had been specially chosen, for reasons she couldn't comprehend, chosen as its sacrifice. It was going to overcome them, devour them in its cold, wet blackness. She wasn't ready, this wasn't right, this wasn't how they were supposed to go. They had been good, upstanding people, people with philosophies, beliefs, ideas they'd lived by. Yes, it had been hard, yes, she'd been lonely, but it had been glorious too. Days in the sun, lying on beaches, walking through forests, picnicking on clifftops covered in rhododendron, overlooking the jumbled roofs of cities. Did all that count for nothing? She had tended her garden. They'd gone to see arthouse films in the cinema. They'd fought, yes, but they'd also touched one another tenderly, had talked and drunk wine. She'd fallen asleep with his arm draped across her stomach, on hundreds, thousands, hundreds of thousands of nights. Death couldn't come like this for people like them. It was absurd. It was unjust, wrong. It had to be wrong. She wasn't ready. The rain beat harder, the wind careened down the chimney, she could hear the tell-tale drips dripping quickly now on the hearth, *thip, thip, thip, thip*. This was all wrong, it couldn't be, not like this, not after all they'd, all still to – *Wake up!* Her body screamed out across the hearth, across the whole world. P*lease, please, please wake up!*

But there was nothing. He, her husband, made no sound, and no one was coming to save them. Outside, through the rain, she could hear the creak of the swaying larches. The air crackled. A storm was approaching from the sea. The sea, the sea itself must be coming. The thought, its finality, soothed her. *Well, of course it is,* she thought, her body growing lax. Her pain, even that was fading. She was so tired. So terribly tired. And why, she wondered, her breaths even shallower than before, had they come here in the first place? Why had they come? She had no idea. It was impossible now to recall, with all that had happened, and with the rain and wind so fast and hard and loud, the romance with which they'd imbued the place. Such stupid fools they'd been. A land of green hills and fairy tales. Of Celtic mists and a lulling, gentle lawlessness. Or so they'd thought. An untethered sort of place, where he'd said she would be able to paint, unhampered by the constraints of English society, and where he could write his poems, like Yeats. Where they could drink pints of Guinness amongst but set apart from the simple existence of the locals, observing, listening, gleaning essential information on life's basic truths, remembered here by these honest, uncomplicated people, so far from the ugliness of modernity. Where, they'd imagined, they could of an evening listen to Atlantic winds whistling gently as they read their books by the fire, or make soft, familiar love in their Victorian, iron-wrought bed. Yes, they'd had some notion of achieving the final stage of their independence here, the aim around which their whole life together had been structured. They'd decided on this waylaid place because they'd wanted to live far from the usual petty concerns of the world. They'd wanted to be free of it all. And free they had become.

Hours, days, lifetimes later. Water lapped soundlessly around her feet. All was perfect silence.

'Harry?' she called across the lake of their living room.

'Yes, love?' she heard him answer.

'Are we dying now?'

Her nostrils filled with the scent of her favourite yellow roses, the ones she grew under the kitchen window in her old garden. But they bloomed in June – what were those roses doing here, now, in October? She didn't understand.

It was so dark and yet, and yet – there he was. She could see him now, her husband. Her partner, her one, lifelong love, healthy brown and glistening blue. Cherry for his cherry, that's what he'd said. He was smiling. He leaned forward out of his chair to meet her. He took her hand and squeezed it. She watched as he opened his mouth to answer.

Acknowledgements

I would like to thank the Arts Council of Ireland, without whose support this book would not exist.

I would very much like to thank all those at Banshee Press, particularly Laura Cassidy and Eimear Ryan, without whose faith and diligent work this book might, in a lesser form, exist, but would have likely remained nothing more than a document on my computer.

Finally, I would like to thank my husband, David Fagleman, for all the above, and the rest.

Banshee Press was founded by writers Laura Cassidy, Claire Hennessy and Eimear Ryan. Since 2015, *Banshee* literary journal has appeared twice a year.

The Banshee Press imprint launched in 2019, publishing the very best in new fiction, poetry and memoir. Banshee Press authors include Bebe Ashley, Dylan Brennan, Gustav Parker Hibbett, Mary Morrissy, Deirdre Sullivan, Rosamund Taylor and David Toms.

WWW.BANSHEEPRESS.ORG